DROWNED BOY

Drowned Boy

by Jerry Gabriel

Winner of the 2008
Mary McCarthy Prize in Short Fiction
Selected by Andrea Barrett

Sarabande  Books

LOUISVILLE, KENTUCKY

FIRST EDITION

Library of Congress Cataloging-in-Publication Data

Gabriel, Jerry, 1969–
    Drowned boy : stories / by Jerry Gabriel. — 1st ed.
        p.   cm.
    ISBN 978-1-932511-78-9 (pbk. : alk. paper)
    1. Middle West—Social life and customs—Fiction. I. Title.
    PS3607.A255D76 2010
    813'.6—dc22   2009005161

ISBN-13: 978-1-932511-78-9

Cover and text design by Charles Casey Martin

Manufactured in Canada
This book is printed on acid-free paper.

Sarabande Books is a nonprofit literary organization.

The Kentucky Arts Council, the state arts agency, supports Sarabande
Books with state tax dollars and federal funding from the National
Endowment for the Arts.

For Karen

CONTENTS

ACKNOWLEDGMENTS

I would like to thank the editors of the various magazines and journals in which these stories have appeared, including the folks at *Elysian Fields Quarterly*, *The Tampa Tribune*, *Cottonwood*, *Writers' Forum*, *Fiction*, *Epoch* and *One Story*, as well as *Punch and Pie: A Short Story Anthology* (Gorsky Press). Joe Martin and Michael Koch at *Epoch* and Hannah Tinti at *One Story* particularly helped me fully realize the stories they published.

I would also like to thank the many, many folks who have helped me out with these stories along the way. In no particular order, these people are: Ana Maria Spagna, Jim Ruland, Gregory Downs, Tom White, Tim Croft, Amity Gaige, Mark Rader, Patrick Somerville, Ben Warner, George McCormick, Katherine Fausset, Stuart Dybek, Brett Navin, Pat Navin, Petter Nordal, Mark Iwinski, Amy Spencer, Erik Stump, Jon Tompkins, Rick Evans, Jennifer Cognard-Black, Matt Hall, James Kessler, Karen Olson, Sean Carswell, Felizon Vidad, Todd Taylor, Stephen Schottenfeld, Siobhan Adcock, Andrew Roth, Sam White, Gillian Kiley, Sally Keith, Jonathan Levy, Lyrae Van Clief-Stefanon, Anette Schwarz, Ted Lee, Tim Watt, Matt Boone, Will Hacker, Maggie Vandermeer, Ann Cummins, Lee K. Abbott, Barry Unsworth, Barbara Anderson, Donley Watt, Marilynne Robinson, and Ethan Canin. I am thankful, too, for a generous grant The New York Foundation for the Arts gave me to help with the completion of the manuscript. I want to thank my family-Greg and Cheryl Arnett, Stacey Arnett, Lisa Wood, Doug Gabriel, and Normal Gabriel-as well as my wife's family-Greg and Mona Anderson, and Amy Swanson-for their unwavering support. And finally, I want to thank my wife Karen for her belief in me and in this book.

FOREWORD

In this spare, sturdy collection, place—the municipality of Moraine, Ohio, home to glacial valleys and a decrepit high school, a single highway connecting it to the outside world and a slowly snaking river that once ran one way, and now runs the other—links the stories, powerfully shaping the characters' lives. Among them are coaches, teachers, high-school students, parents, the avid fans of an elementary school basketball team, a grieving family, and many more. But although the stories are told from a variety of perspectives, all have to do, directly or indirectly, with two brothers, Nate and Donnie Holland, and this place in which they come of age.

Nate, who narrates several of the stories and is the point-of-view character in several others, is eight years old when the collection opens and twenty-four when it closes. During those sixteen years, the changes he experiences are mirrored by those taking place in what was once an isolated and largely rural community. Even as a young child, Nate dreaded that his beloved older brother, Donnie, would leave him:

> His brother was going to run off again—someday possibly for good.
> Nate lay awake for a long time trying not to imagine, but then
> imagining anyway, life when Donnie disappeared.

When Donnie fulfills that prophecy, his departure leaves Nate adrift in a post-industrial heartland stripped of its old stability. There are broken relationships, broken cars, a tornado—"This is a damn mess," one character says. "I can abide all sorts of things, but I do not care for tornadoes"—and drunken men shooting cans off fence posts. In the present, "many of us had fallen into our lives in the months and years leading up to that time—an abysmal rut of receptionist by day and movie renter by night. It was monotony. We were beaten down, really, gaining weight in unproud ways." Of the past, only unreliable relics remain: Nate's dead father's watch, for example, which is "junky and about forty years old" and "did a poor job of telling time and did so with little sliding digits like most watches use only for the date."

As it goes for Nate, so it goes for Moraine and, by extension, for the rest of us as well. These stories are filled with boys, poised between one state and the next: not just Nate and Donnie but a runaway boy, a lost boy, a beaten boy, a clever boy—and, of course, the drowned boy of the excellent title novella. He remains offstage, leaving Nate, newly out of high school, and a classmate named Samantha, to vibrate to the consequences of his death. But although we never meet him, his drowning resonates metaphorically through the collection. In Moraine, Nate's entire generation seems to be in danger of sinking beneath the water.

These are rust-belt blues, then, a vision of and lament for a past time and a swiftly changing place. They're not showy—the language is plain, the tragedy muted, the comedy low-key and wry—but they stick in the mind. Raymond Carver would recognize these characters and situations, as would poet Philip Levine. I like to think that that they would share my appreciation for this fine first book, built slowly and carefully over some years, and worth the wait.

—Andrea Barrett

DROWNED BOY

Boys Industrial School

THE DEPUTY SEEMED TO BE MEASURING THE BOYS UP. He looked away from them, up and down the road from the seat of his cruiser, his window down. Beyond Nate and Donnie Holland there was just the desolate November woods and the endless hills and Milford Run meandering next to the road among its thickets. It was chilly and they wore heavy coats; their breath billowed in front of them.

"Boy run off Thursday from the Industrial School," the deputy told them. "Neither a you seen a blond-headed kid, 'bout your age?" He was looking at Donnie. Donnie was twelve.

"No sir. Ain't seen anybody out today."

"Your parents home, are they?"

They were quiet for a moment. "Mom," Nate started to say, but then stopped there. Their father had been in the hospital for the better part of two weeks, but Nate could think of no good way to explain this and could think of no reason why it would matter to the deputy. "We live in the green house down the bottom of the hill," he said. He wanted to make sure the deputy understood that they themselves were not runaways. Nate was just eight.

The deputy sat there for a long, awkward time. He pulled a red cigarette pack from his shirt pocket and tapped one out and lit it.

Nate knew about the Boys' Industrial School. BIS, they called it. It was up Milford Run a ways, fifteen miles or more—an old, beautiful red building with an arched entryway. It looked as if it had surely been built for some purpose other than detaining juvenile delinquents. Nate had always thought it looked like it belonged in Italy or France, based on pictures of those places he'd seen in his *Societies of the World* textbook. Except for the high chain-link fence and razor wire. Guards patrolled the grounds and there was a single cylindrical tower from which, his brother had told him, they shot at runaways. Boys there wore blue coveralls. Sometimes they were out on the grounds or even along the roadsides working.

The deputy seemed to make a decision. He put the car into gear and it idled faster as he held his foot on the brake.

"That's a mean boy I'm looking for," he told them. "You all be careful."

"Yessir," Donnie said.

"All right."

He pulled away slowly, eyeing them cautiously in his rearview mirror.

An hour later, they'd stolen pops from the out-building behind the Howards' place and were squatting in a culvert along the creek. The water trickled, a spartan winter flow. It was snowing now—hard for November. They opened their pops on a birch stump and drank them as they plotted how to find the boy.

Donnie said they should borrow a few of the horses on the other side of the ridge. They would need them to track with, he said. Not steal them. Just take them out for a while.

"You ever rode a horse bareback before?" Nate asked.

"Shoot yeah," Donnie said. "Me and Riley used to ride them horses over at Williams' all the time." It was just enough plausible detail.

"Do you think there'll be a reward for the boy?" Nate asked.

"Bingo," Donnie said. "Somebody give the smart kid a prize."

There was already an inch of snow on the ground when they dropped down within sight of Lape's meadow. The field looked whiter than anything else, long stems of pale grass poking through.

"What if they buck us?" Nate asked.

"You hang on, wrap your arms around tight," Donnie said. "They're good horses."

"Yeah, but what if they don't want us on them?"

"They don't mind," Donnie said. "That's what they're for."

Nate waited under a juniper while Donnie went to find the horses. He could smell the coal issue from the Lape's chimney on down the hill.

Soon he saw something emerge, and then another something, and another. It was the horses, galloping at first and then stopping and looking around themselves. Donnie was behind them with a branch in his hand. Nate got up and walked toward his brother, and the three horses stood anxiously nearby and feigned eating the snow-covered grass.

"I'll take that paint there," Donnie said.

"Which one should I take?"

"Go for the little one. The brown one."

Donnie approached his horse, talking to it all the while. "Hey there, Mister. I ain't gonna do nothing." Nate watched, waited.

He reached down and picked up a handful of the grass and held it out as he neared the horse. The animal took anxious side steps, but did not run. Donnie extended the grass and it finally bent its head toward the grass and chewed. The boy began to pet its mane and its nose. The horse stared at him impassively when it had finished eating. Donnie was talking to it still and then he stepped back and almost in the same motion, rushed forward and grabbed a fistful of mane and leaped toward its back. The horse bucked and kicked as Donnie fell to the ground, its rear legs just missing his shoulder.

"She-it," Donnie said, picking himself up. The horse ran a few steps away and looked back in the direction of the boys.

"Come on," Nate said. "We ain't gonna be able to ride these horses."

"She-it." Donnie brushed the snow off his coat. He was looking at all three horses now. "Snow probably scares 'em."

On the way home, Nate slipped into a deep spot in Milford Run up to his knee. Donnie couldn't stop laughing. "Mr. Straight-As," he said. "That last step's a doozy."

"Shut up," Nate said. He left the creek, crawled by himself through twenty yards of bushes to the road and then walked toward home.

A half hour later, his mom was helping him get his pants off.

"Where's you're brother?" she asked.

"I don't know," he told her.

It was almost dark when Donnie came back. Nate was watching television. He was still mad and wouldn't speak to Donnie. Soon, their mother called them into the kitchen to eat tuna casserole, and the three of them sat there quietly eating while the sober voice of AM radio news drifted through the room.

The boys shared a big room on the second floor and their beds ran parallel, about ten feet apart. They each had a small plastic radio—Donnie's was blue, Nate's red—with a single white earphone that fit into one ear and plugged into a jack on the radio. After the lights were out, Nate liked to listen to his as loud as it would go. The boom of radio voices flitted about in the dark. Donnie never complained, though. He never complained about anything.

Nate often listened to WLW out of Cincinnati, but it didn't matter, really; he'd listen to whatever would come in. Sometimes it was hockey from out West—Denver or Calgary—or a sports talk show from Chicago. He caught Ohio University playing Marshall at the Convocation Center. He memorized players' names and eventually got the Encyclopedia out and learned the geography of the region this way.

When the boys split up into teams during recess, Eric Stimson would always yell, "We're the Buckeyes."

"So," Nate yelled back one day. "We're the Thundering Herd." He loved that name.

"That's stupid. There ain't no such thing."

Nate shrugged. There was such a thing as the Thundering Herd, he said. They played for a university called Marshall. Marshall University was in Huntington, West Virginia. West Virginia bordered Ohio on the southeast. Its capital was Charleston. Its major export was coal. It was known as "the Mountain State."

"I don't care about any of that," Stimson said, but Nate's team liked the idea of being something beside the hapless Buckeyes, who were having a particularly bad season that year anyway.

"Yeah," a fourth grader said. "We're the Thundering Herd." He stomped his feet like a one-man stampede. "Now kick us the dang ball."

Nate wrote about this in his journal. The book had been a Christmas gift from their father and it had a lock and key. Sometimes Donnie picked it with a pen knife. He held it up high and recited sections out loud. "Last night I dreamed me and Cara was getting chased by robbers. We found a note someone wrote us, but it was in French or Russian. I read it anyway. It said to hide behind Foodtown." Nate would have to fight him to get it back.

Donnie stole the journal often enough that Nate stopped writing about his own thoughts, and instead began making up stories about his brother. *Donnie talks all night in his sleep. Donnie snores. Donnie farts so loud at night it wakes me up. Sometimes he walks all around the house in his sleep, screaming about monsters under his bed and crying for Daddy.* It worked. His brother left the journal alone and Nate was able to keep his secrets again.

They set out early the next day, a Sunday. Donnie said the trip would not be for the weak. He knew a place where they'd probably find the boy, an abandoned village up in the woods called Clayville. It was a ways, he said.

"What're we going to do when we catch him?" Nate asked.

"Tie him up, numbnuts," Donnie said. "March him to someone's house and call the Sheriff."

"We got any rope?"

Donnie pulled a forty-foot section of twine from his pack.

"What if he's big?"

"We'll be able to take him," Donnie said. "There's two of us."

They packed sandwiches and fruit and brownies and little quarts of milk Donnie had stolen from school. Donnie went through the back of the pantry and found some crackers and peanut butter. They also had some old C-rations they'd gotten from their cousin who was in the National Guard.

It was warmer out today, and they soon tied their coats around their waists. They walked quietly. Donnie operated in two modes, and didn't shift well between them. He was either silent for great lengths of time, or he was talking non-stop. Nate had learned to accept this, and when Donnie was silent, he was silent, too.

They followed the creek at first. There was an animal trail there, but they had to cross the stream a lot, stepping on fallen trees and midstream rocks. In a few places, they jumped where it was deep and narrow with a high cutbank, the water hardly moving beneath them. They landed on the other side and rolled. Always Donnie first.

At the Pederson's they cut toward the ridge to the west and hiked up the hill and over the top to the next valley over. They could hear Shepard and Mollie, the McCaslin's coon dogs, howling from where they were chained next to the old trailer the family lived in.

When they finally stopped to rest, Nate opened his pack to find something to eat. Donnie pulled out a pack of cigarettes and smoked one.

"Where'd you get those?"

"Store in Perry." He acted like he'd been smoking them his whole life.

"Mom'll smell it on you."

"Mom don't know squat," Donnie said.

Nate shrugged and stared at the smoke coming from his brother's nose.

"Come on," Donnie said, getting up. "We've got some miles to cover."

"Along the ridge up here for a while," Donnie said as they walked on, gesturing with a nod of his head, a mannerism he'd picked up from their father, who'd used it to indicate the direction of some approaching weather, say, or the location of his truck in a crowded parking lot.

Despite poor grades and poor behavior reports—despite all that suggested universal incompetence—Donnie possessed an infallible natural compass; he navigated like a bird. For Nate, it was like another language, this ability. He'd been told that moss grows on the north sides of trees and that you could find your way by signs, but Donnie wasn't using moss or any other kind of tool or trick. He just knew.

They moved along at a steady pace for a few hours, but the march was wearing Nate down. While climbing over a fence, he lost concentration and caught his leg between a branch and the wire. He teetered there for a long moment and then fell, head first, to the other side, able at the last moment to get his arm below him to catch himself with, but the weight of his body coming down was too much for the arm, and he wrenched it. The pain shot through him like a current and for a long moment he was inconsolable, his brain too overloaded to even register his brother's questions about breakage and where it hurt.

He lay face down, his head in a pile of wet leaves. He screamed and pressed his arm against the damp earth and clenched his entire body as if expecting another fall. "Calm down," Donnie was telling him. "You're okay."

Donnie took off his pack and untied his coat and then pulled off his shirt. He tore part of it up and made a sling.

Soon, he was able to sit Nate up and lean him against a tree. He doctored Nate's arm, putting the sling on him, tying it close to his body.

"You're doing good, Little Man," he was saying. "We're close now. You're gonna be all right."

Nate was crying. He knew he could make Donnie take him back.

"We gonna do this?" Donnie said at last, smiling.

Nate nodded. Donnie picked up both packs and carried them now.

They came out of the woods less than a half hour later onto a dirt bike trail. Deep tire canals furrowed into the ground, lightly frozen in the weather. The path led to a series of ruined buildings: Clayville. A sign nailed to a tree said so. It was an old gold mining camp, Donnie told him. It did look like an abandoned camp, but Nate knew that there'd been no gold here and that if it was a mining camp, it was probably salt or coal.

Donnie dropped the packs near a rock and disappeared into one of the doorways. Nate sat down and found some crackers and began eating, careful not to agitate his arm. Soon Donnie came back and sat beside him and opened a can of C-rations—beans and wieners.

"What'd you find?" he asked.

"Nobody here," he said.

"What should we do?"

Donnie shrugged and seemed to take the first step toward drifting into impassivity, his senses of the outside world seemingly shutting down. He watched TV that way, and you needed to turn it off to get his attention.

In one of the buildings there was some noise. "Donnie," Nate said, and he shoved him. His brother had pulled a book from his jacket—a Western—and lit a cigarette.

There was some more noise, a door opened, and the blond convict emerged. He approached them through the middle of the camp, what the miners—if there had been miners—had probably called Broad or Main Street. He was, like the deputy had said, about Donnie's size. He wore blue coveralls that were ratty and muddy in patches. The uniform lent him the look of an overworked mechanic. His head was shorn in what had once been a crew cut, but the hair had grown out and now stood on end, not long enough yet to lay down. He had freckles and his face was straight, almost somber, as he neared.

"The convict," Nate said. Donnie did not even seem to hear him.

When he was close enough not to yell, he called out, "I bum a 'rette?"

Donnie looked up now, calmly, as if looking up at a sunset someone was calling his attention to. He nodded and, when the boy was closer, he threw him the pack and the lighter. The boy caught both, each with his right hand, and proceeded to maneuver a cigarette out and light it. He crouched near where they were sitting, catcher-style. He reeked of earth and sweat. He smelled, Nate thought, like the inside of the barn.

"What you guys doing up here?" he asked.

"Scoutin' deer," Donnie said.

"A hunter, are you?"

"Last year was my first," Donnie said. "Little man here's too young yet."

The boy nodded. "I got a nine-point buck last winter down toward Lawrence County," he said.

"Yeah?" Donnie said. "We seen a twelve-point not two miles that way."

Everything that came out of his brother's mouth was a lie, Nate thought. His brother's inner-workings, he thought, were no better understood to him than those of his transistor radio.

He sat and watched the two boys—the criminal and his brother—as if they were a movie and he was waiting to see what would happen next. Nate was terrified and the boy seemed to know it, cautiously taking glances at him during the conversation.

"Ya'll from nearby?" he asked.

"Down Milford Run Road a way," Donnie told him. His brother seemed impossibly comfortable, smoking the last of his cigarette, his Western novel in his other hand. "Where you from?"

"Portsmouth, man. It's a good long morning's drive from here. I just been over to BIS since last April. I run off the other day during road crew. Had all I could take."

"That's why you got the nice blue suit there?" Donnie said.

"Yeah," the boy said. It was hard to tell if he was annoyed or ashamed.

"What are you gonna do?" Nate asked.

"Little Man speaks," he said to the ground, and spat. Then he looked at Nate. "What do you care? You workin' for the High Sheriff?"

"No," Nate said.

The boy looked back down. "I'll probably hitch a ride down to Oklahoma. I got some relation down there."

They were all quiet for a time.

"You ain't got any food in your pack, do you?" the boy said.

"Hell, son," Donnie said. "It's like a damn grocery in there." He opened it and pulled out what they had left. "You got your peanut butter sandwiches. Bananas. Brownies. A little crackers left."

The boy took what Donnie handed him. "Thanks," he said. "I been starvin' out here. And freezin'. I ain't been able to start a fire. No Boy Scout. I'll tell you that."

The boy ate everything they had.

After a time Nate went to the woods to go to the bathroom. As he came back he heard the boy ask about him.

"Nate?" Donnie said. "He's alright. I gotta get him home before his bedtime, though."

"Just gotta be careful, you know," the boy said. "How far is it to the highway, you reckon?"

"Long way," Donnie said. "Probably five mile."

"That way?" He pointed toward the west.

"Nah," Donnie said. "You'll want to head that way." He was pointing north.

"I walk with you guys, you be able to sneak me some food later on? And some matches?"

"Sure," Donnie said. "I an get you all the stuff you want."

"What about a road map?"

"Yeah," Donnie said. "There's a stack of maps downstairs nobody pays any attention to."

"All right," he said.

Nate decided to join them again.

"What's a matter with your arm, Little Man?" the boy asked, noticing the sling.

"I fell," Nate said.

"It broke or something?"

Nate shook his head and felt ashamed. He tested the limb with his good arm and it felt fine now, and he pulled the sling off. "It's better," he said. The boy laughed.

"Let's go," Donnie said, and the three of them started walking toward the ramshackle farmhouse in silence. It had taken the boys a long time to get out there, and now they would be pushing it to get back before dark.

The sky clouded up and the weather turned colder. When they rested, Donnie passed the cigarettes over and the boy told them about BIS.

"They got you picking up trash?" Donnie asked.

"Yeah, they always got us doing something. Sometimes it's building bridges on trails or digging ditches for culverts or raking leaves."

"What are the other kids like?" Nate asked.

He shrugged. "They're just kids," he said. "Like at school pretty much."

"There fights?" Nate asked.

"Some."

"Anybody get stabbed?"

"Where you getting these questions, Little Man?"

"I just heard at school that a kid got stabbed at BIS."

"Nobody I seen," the boy said. "They don't let you eat with real silverware."

"What did you do to get sent there?" Nate asked, getting bolder.

"I killed a kid with my dad's 30 aught," he said.

Donnie looked at the boy and Nate looked at Donnie. The boy laughed. "I'm just foolin' around," he said. "I stole a truck and wrecked it."

"That all?" Donnie said.

"No," the boy said. "I stole some bike parts from a store back home and I also threw a desk out of a window at school to see what would happen."

"What happened?" Nate asked.

"It exploded on the cement just like you'd think it would. But a leg broke off and caught a guidance counselor in the ass. That was the real problem."

Nate didn't ask anymore questions. He was wondering how someone comes to be the kind of person who steals things and smashes them and runs away. The line between doing those things and not didn't seem altogether clear.

Donnie and Nate left the blond boy at one of their forts in the pines. Nate didn't speak until they were almost to the yard.

"What are we gonna do?"

"Sittin' duck, ain't he?" Donnie said.

For a moment, Nate couldn't believe how good Donnie had been. He was as calm as some TV undercover cop.

"We call the sheriff?" Nate asked.

"No," Donnie said. "Not yet. You just act like nothing happened. It's easy. Mom asks, you just tell her we took a long hike up into the woods."

Nate nodded. "Why?"

"Because he'll be on the lookout for a setup tonight. I'll bring him out some food and then we'll call the pigs in the morning. He'll still be asleep and we'll lead them right to him."

Inside their mom was watching TV.

"The lost have returned," she said.

She ordered baths before dinner. If they wanted to see the Sunday Night Movie, they'd have to hurry.

The three of them ate in front of the TV. A rare treat. *Herbie Goes to Monte Carlo*. Because of the excitement of the adventure, of the long hike and finding the boy, Nate hadn't even thought of his dad all day. But now that the three of them sat in front of the television, his absence became glaring. He thought of asking his mom if she'd heard anything, but she seemed content just then and he didn't want to spoil that.

Later that night Nate was listening to the BBC in bed. He noticed Donnie getting dressed.

"You going out there now?" Nate asked.

"Uh huh."

Nate sat up.

"Should I come with you?"

Donnie laughed. "You wuss," he said. "It would take Coxey's Army to get you out into the woods tonight."

"No," Nate said. "I'll go. We're in this together, ain't we?"

"Yeah," Donnie said. "We're in it together. You do your part and cover for me if mom comes in."

"How?"

"Tell her I'm in the bathroom. I don't know. You're supposed to be the smart one."

Nate nodded. And then Donnie was gone out the window, onto the roof over the porch where he could easily jump down to the ground, and Nate eventually got tired of waiting up for him and nodded off.

The next morning Donnie's bed was empty. He wasn't in the kitchen when Nate came down for breakfast.

"Donnie!" their mom yelled up the stairs. She turned to Nate. "Where's your brother?"

He froze. "I don't know."

"He upstairs?"

"He wasn't in his bed."

She went upstairs and then came back down.

"Where is your brother?"

He shook his head.

She went outside and yelled for Donnie again, then came back in. Nate ate a bowl of cereal.

"Get ready for the bus," she told him. "Brush your teeth."

Nate did as he was told. As he was sitting tying his shoes he thought, what if Donnie was in trouble? He should tell, he decided, and then he changed his mind back. And then back again. He was still running in this loop sitting on the bus on the way to school. The bus lumbered on up Milford Run Road, climbing into the hills with seeming pain. It was cold. Winter had finally come for good.

The road turned west toward town before they went far enough to see BIS and Nate imagined the place as he remembered it, piecing together the brief glimpses he'd had. Sitting in his seat, he quietly resigned himself to whatever came. He would play ignorant until he couldn't anymore. It didn't make any sense that Donnie would go with the boy, but maybe he had.

That night, when Donnie didn't show up after school, Nate heard their mother call the Sheriff's department and report him missing; there was a wrecked quality in her voice, a despondence he wished he could right. But he didn't have any idea how he might do this, and telling her about Donnie and the blond boy would only make it worse.

After she called the Sheriff, she sat out on the front porch in the cold, as if she could get a better view of the world from out there. Nate lay on his bed and waited. All of the possible explanations felt unreal. They were almost not possibilities at all, but absurdities—that his brother had been hurt or killed or had run off, or most improbable of all, had gotten lost somehow out there in the dark and was even now wandering around the big woods, searching for some clue of where he was.

Two days later, Donnie came back. He was alone and he was dirty and he himself smelled of leaves and dirt. Their mother pulled Donnie to her and held him tightly before she hit him, once on the neck. Then she called the Sheriff's Department to tell them that Donnie was okay.

At around eight that night the deputy who had questioned them on the road pulled into their driveway. He spoke to Donnie in the kitchen. Nate listened from the TV room.

"Where you been these last few days?" the Sheriff asked.

"I was up in the woods," Donnie told him. "Thought I'd camp out."

"In November?"

"I don't know. Ain't nothin' ever just grabbed you and then you just did it?"

The man sighed.

"Did you come across this boy?" He was probably holding up a photograph of the blond kid.

"Never saw no one."

"Where did you go?"

"Told you. I was just camping up in the woods. I can show you where."

The deputy sent Donnie away and talked to their mom outside. Their voices were low and their mother closed the front door quietly as the engine of his patrol car started up.

Later, when the boys were lying in bed, Donnie said, "Good job, buddy."

"For what?" Nate asked.

"For not ratting."

Nate was quiet. "I was scared," he said. "I thought that boy might've killed you or something. What happened?"

"I changed my mind about ole boy. I took him to the highway."

"Why?"

"I don't know. Just felt like it."

"I thought we was going to turn him in," Nate said.

"No," Donnie said. "He ain't no criminal."

"How do you know?"

Donnie was quiet for a minute. Then he said, in a tone of finality, "You can tell a criminal."

He turned over and pulled the covers over his head. Nate was still mad, though.

"Donnie," he whispered a few minutes later.

His brother breathed lightly, sleeping.

"Donnie," Nate said, louder this time.

"Yeah?"

"Why'd you help that boy escape?"

Donnie didn't answer, though, and Nate knew he wouldn't. He imagined his brother running off again—someday possibly for good. Nate lay awake for a long time trying not to imagine, but then imagining anyway, life when Donnie disappeared. There seemed no preparation for that, no way of bracing himself.

"Donnie?" he heard himself say. He could not close his eyes. It was not dread exactly, but it resembled it, anticipated it. He called his brother's name again, and then once more. He waited, but nothing, it seemed, was going to bring his brother back from the sleep he'd already entered.

Falling Water

THE BIG FARM HOUSE WAS DIRTY AND WHITE with its paint chipping. Bare lumber showed through in places, dark from the rain, and rusted, dilapidated cars filled the muddy yard, parked anywhere there was space.

Grandpa stood on the porch wearing a Cincinnati Reds cap, his eyes drawn deep into his head. He held a box of Pabst Blue Ribbon beer under his arm. When we got close enough, he smiled. "Hola," he said.

Mom straightened out her dress with her hands and said "Hello, there," but in a quiet voice, the way she had talked while Dad had been in the hospital. Dad and Donnie and I all stood quietly behind her. Dad looked toward the hills, like he might be searching for something there, while Grandpa and Mom said a few words about the weather. Donnie ran off through the yard until Dad, still holding the casserole dish, yelled, "Get back over here." And Donnie did, right away. Dad had little patience in those months and we learned to listen to him the first time. Donnie had run away in August, and when he was turned in two days later by a family fifteen miles away, hungry and dirty, I worried that Dad might actually kill him. He beat him out in front of the barn, first with a switch and then with his fists, and Donnie's wails carried across our entire farm, Dad's guttural questions two octaves lower.

A door opened behind Grandpa and I could hear voices for a second, and then a small woman appeared and the door slammed behind her. She walked over to Grandpa's side and he wrapped his arm around her. She was much younger than him—twenty-six years younger, I learned later—and she was short, coming just to the crook of his elbow. Grandpa said to Mom—or maybe to of all of us—"Like ye to meet Shirley." He smiled for a minute, and his teeth showed, and I could see a couple that were dark or missing.

Mom walked up the steps to the porch and shook the woman's hand and said, "Nice to meet you." After a brief moment during which everyone stood awkwardly still, Grandpa turned around toward us again, taking Shirley by the elbow, and he introduced us, one at a time, without hesitating, like our names were as common to his tongue as *pass the butter*; but this was only the second time I'd seen the man in my life. The first had been two years back, when he showed up at our farm and reentered my mother's life after nearly a forty-year absence.

During this introduction, Shirley stayed on the porch and we stayed in the grass and Donnie and I nodded to the young woman just the way Dad did.

Grandpa and Shirley led us through the peeling front door, and into the first room, which was a huge country kitchen. Inside, a dozen or so women moved about frenetically, preparing Thanksgiving supper, and Grandpa stashed the new beer in a rounded refrigerator in a corner.

Some of the women smiled at us as Mom pushed me and Donnie through the kitchen into a room where Dallas played Houston on a black-and-white television and a roomful of men sat on torn chairs and couches. They were heartily drinking Genesee and Pabst and had a coffee table full of empties to prove it.

"These are your relations," Mom told me, as if it were the single most important facet of being alive. She pulled off my coat and hung it in a large closet Grandpa had shown her. I knew that she had read my mind as she sometimes could and there was not going to be any fussing about it.

She disappeared into the kitchen. In the living room Grandpa inquired about the score and introduced Dad in nearly the same breath. A man in bib overalls said there was no score. I watched as Dad leaned into a dark corner, tightly holding the can of beer Grandpa had given him, glancing at the television. The men looked up from the game briefly to see what Dad looked like and then immediately returned their attention to an incomplete pass on the screen.

Donnie and I stood near a boy and girl sitting on the floor playing an adult board game. "What's a membrane?" the girl asked us, looking at a small card she held in her hand, as if the question were a perfectly reasonable one and we might be in possession of the answer. I shrugged and Donnie, uninterested, moved toward some other kids; there was upward of a dozen of kids in various parts of the house.

I stood and watched the game for a minute and listened to the mumble of the men in the adjacent room. When I finally moved, I saw that Donnie had already made friends with two kids playing *Risk*; they were dressed almost exactly like us. I moved away from them and sat for a long time in the empty corridor, carefully running an anonymous Matchbox ambulance back and forth on the stairs. The noise of strangers filled the place and I was thinking again of the day Donnie had run away. To hell with it, he'd told me the morning before he'd left. He'd had enough. If some men hunting squirrel hadn't been found him camped in a cave along Salt Creek one morning, he'd told me later, he would've put some real distance between himself and us.

A loud call came from the kitchen finally and everyone formed a line that stretched back through the hall and into the television room. We had our plates handed to us one at a time, like at school, and these women who wore long dresses and had their hair up stood across the table and scooped things onto our plates for us.

I sat on the floor with my food and listened to the men talk about what Houston should have done on a fourth down and inches. Everyone except Grandpa agreed that they made the right move by going up the middle, even though they didn't get the first down. Grandpa disagreed. "Can't run head-on into something like that," he said. "You got the element of surprise with the pass. When they're expecting one thing, you just go for it all. You go downtown."

After the game, the men filed outside. With the rest of the women upstairs looking at a bridal gown one of them would soon be wearing, my Mom and Shirley stood by themselves in the kitchen, leaning up against the countertop. "Go outside," she told us when Donnie and I came into the room, tired, ready to go home. I could tell that she was tired too. I watched Shirley while Mom talked to us, watched the way she looked at Mom and held her coffee and sipped from it. With the two of them standing beside each other then, I thought that Mom might even have been a little older, which I knew was strange. As it turned out, they were exactly the same age.

Outside, the men were drunk. Their language loosened and a man in a beard and flannel shirt swore at his kids to get off an old Ford tractor that sat next to a barn. A few of the men laughed and sang a silly country song while they set empty beer cans on top of the fence posts separating the yard from a pasture. There was a light drizzle and the sky had turned the dark color of the hillsides. In the yard everything was wet, and the creek ran high just beyond the fence. Donnie and I stood near a corner of the house by ourselves, our hands in our pockets. Next to us, water dripped from a rusted rainspout into an overflowing metal bucket.

Several more of the men came through the back door and stood on the small porch, surveying things for a moment. The porch was crowded already with boxes of pop bottles and tin trash cans, and it seemed like the added weight might push the floor through. Four of them carried rifles.

Dad was in the back of the group. He held a beer in one hand and the other was stuffed into the pocket of his jacket. When the rest of them moved from the porch, he took a seat on the wet boards of the top step.

Grandpa and another man pulled lawn chairs into the yard and sat down, placing their beers in the damp grass beside them. Everybody seemed unaware of the rain, or just unbothered, and the men with guns lined up twenty yards from the target and started shooting at the cans. Every third or fourth shot, a can would fall from a post into the creek and would bob in the water until it disappeared behind an old shed and high grass. The men cheered each shot at first, milling about while they waited their turn, ribbing each other, chatting loudly.

I moved next to Dad on the steps and Donnie stepped closer to the men with the guns, obviously hoping to get his chance. Dad and I sat quietly for what seemed a long time and the shooting continued rapidly, like a small battle nearby. Even if the quiet was too much, I resigned myself to staying there as long as he did. He took slow drinks from the tin can in his hand while a man ran out to the fence, holding his hands up and yelling, "Cease fire, cease fire." He put up new cans in place of the ones that had fallen and then retreated again behind the firing lines.

Grandpa had a gun now, aiming the thing haphazardly, shooting from his lawn chair—from his hip—like some arrogant mercenary. I listened to the muffled echo of his shots as they flew past the cans and into the pasture and I thought about my mother when she was my age, how her father had disappeared. I didn't know anything of the Depression, of course—just that one day she had a father and the next she didn't.

After a spate of poor shooting, Grandpa gave out a final laugh at his bad aim and pointed the gun toward the wet grass at his feet, wedging it under his right arm.

Over near the corncribs and parked cars, a group of women appeared, and I could see Shirley pointing things out to them—flower gardens and a dead tree struck by lightning. When another man knocked down three cans in three shots, he turned to the women and bowed foolishly, awarding himself contest champion. The women giggled and one of them—probably it was his wife—ridiculed him.

Grandpa turned then, after he had the gun loaded again, to give someone else a try, and my brother held out his hands for it. But Grandpa looked over his head and directly toward me and my dad. "Come here and try yer hand at this, Art," he said above the noise, and a lot of the men looked our way. Dad waved him off, though, and stared at his beer. But everyone looked then, including some of the women. The men started in on him. "Come on, Art," they said.

He swore under his breath, and, setting the can between us, stood up. He looked down at me, just before he walked away. He wore an expression I'd never seen from him before, one I interpreted as the communication of a promise; he would hit this can and then everything would be back to normal.

He limped toward Grandpa, holding his arms at his sides, placing each step slowly on the wet ground before taking another. When he finally got there, he took the gun and, holding it down, looked across the yard to the can that rested on top of the old, worn post. He raised the gun to his shoulder. I could see only half of his face and couldn't tell if he squinted to see the can or to fight the pain in his chest, but he squinted hard and there seemed to be a silence carrying over the place.

He lowered the gun twice to look at the target. The light rain turned into something a little more then, and some of the men began to pick up their beers and walk toward cover, all the while watching the man with the gun, some of them backpedaling so they could. They moved under the porch and window awnings. A few of them went inside the screen door, but stayed in the foyer to watch.

Dad did not move. The water spotted his jacket, leaving wet patches here and there, and ran down his face, but his eye remained trained, squinting down the long barrel.

In the next instant, the rain picked up another notch, not yet a downpour, but driving, and most of the crowd seemed to give up on him and began running for the doors. I stayed where I was on the top step, though, even when a man told me to get out of the way. I pretended like I didn't hear him and I stared out into the backyard.

When Grandpa went past, he said, "Let's get inside, son," and I didn't say anything to him either, didn't acknowledge his words and scarcely even looked at him with recognition.

The rain moved in from the hills beyond the house then like a terrible swarm of bees. Near the parked cars where the women last were, I saw a figure step forward from underneath the tin roof of an open-air shed, and I knew from the walk and the way her arms crossed her chest that it was my mother. She moved into the rain, and even though nearly everyone else was gone, my father still stood, patient, taking in and holding that last breath before pulling the trigger. And when the rain finally let loose and a thunder clap exploded over the farm, I thought I heard the echo of a rifle shot and I saw what I thought was the empty beer can falling into the water on the other side of the fence and disappearing into the noise of thunder and rain and rushing water.

The rain came down torrentially then, sheets of solid water. I sat under the metal roof but the rain slanted in and caught me anyway, and I looked out into the darkness of the storm, trying to make out what seemed like two people in the middle of the downpour. If it was them that I saw out there, the mysterious people who represented everything I didn't understand about the world and the few things I did, then they were very close then, maybe touching. And I told myself that it was them, and that they were touching.

Marauders

WE TRAVELED LIKE GYPSIES TO THESE LITTLE TOWNS—places called Mudsock and Comersville and just plain Water. Sometimes we set up tarps and cooked hot dogs on fires started inconspicuously in the corner of a parking lot, or back in some small wood where an unnamed brook ran. Because we knew the Marauders would be in the finals, we planned accordingly, stocked up on supplies, took catnaps in Terry Winston's conversion van, located the best diner in town. We'd have a trophy in the end; we knew that. And when we all rolled back into Moraine late, Cooley's would buzz with reveling. There would be things broken, maybe even some minor injuries. But who cared? These things are part of life when you were really living it.

We sat on those uncomfortable wooden bleachers for hours on end—days, sometimes—donning our maroon-and-gold sweaters and polo shirts. We knitted hats and gloves of those colors for our children and grandparents. We smoked under the empty skies in elementary school parking lots at halftime, when you could see all the way to the next galaxy and the cold made you giddy. And afterward we liked to have a quick celebratory swig before driving back to Cooley's where we could celebrate in earnest. Somebody always had a bottle of something or another under the car seat. We gave high fives, sometimes even embraced each other. These were not normal times. We drove recklessly, joyously through the hills and honked our horns to hamlets and empty gas stations, farms and darkness.

Only a few of us had been there in earlier seasons—in the days when the Marauders had worn hand-me-down uniforms and played below .500. Graham Wilson—the old vet who sat in bibbed-overalls and chewed on a perpetual Swisher Sweet—he'd been one of them. He'd followed them for decades into every dinky one-horse town in southeast Ohio, every backwater gym where five opposing boys and a ref could be scrounged up. Late, after we'd returned from a victory, he'd tell stories about it at the bar, of less talented teams, of boys we knew—some now sitting among us—who as men would work for the county road crew, the tile plant, Odd Lots. In these tales there were crooked referees, hostile crowds, buzzer beating jumpers, and always somehow heartbreak, which killed us. It killed us. We loved to listen to Graham Wilson because even if we hadn't been there, they were our stories too. And it was our heartbreak.

One of those stories was in the making one cold February evening, right in the heart of winter, when darkness comes on too early. We made the drive after work and shuffled toward the school from our corps of minivans and Dodge Colts, the vinyl seats cracking under us from the cold. We slapped each other on the back, traded jocular insults. We smoked one last cigarette and then descended the stairs into this CCC-constructed building, ducking to miss the low-hanging asbestos-wrapped pipes.

Great caged phosphorous bulbs lit the gym from above, and we saw immediately, in two neat lines beginning at half-court, our Marauders—the cream of the crop of Moraine's fifth and sixth grade classes—in the middle of one of their elaborate warm-up drills. After watching dozens of times, it still wasn't clear what kind of magic moved them so quickly.

At the other end of the court, a group of ragamuffin boys warmed up clad in white jerseys, many of their numbers in different fonts. One of them wore a pair of boots without socks and had a head of hair in bad need of a brushing. We glanced at one another, suppressing laughs, though something here felt sad, too.

So many of us had fallen into our lives in the months and years leading up to that season—an abysmal rut of receptionist by day and movie renter by night. Monotony. We felt beaten down, really, gaining weight in unproud ways. We lived off Tommy's Pizza and Yankee Burger, Milwaukee's Best, or strawberry daiquiris if we were in a good mood. None of us could've passed as the picture of good living, and we talked nostalgically and too often of the time we'd been to Virginia Beach. It was always, *Remember that little restaurant we found down on that side street near the water? The Outrigger? Pirate Jack's?* And, the reply: *My God did they have good jumbo shrimp.* A confirming nod, a wistful look, a whispered *Damn.* We talked of going again with the knowledge we never would.

And the Marauders, in the heart of their youth, with their shiny maroon and gold uniforms, their snappy warm-up drills, their hustle: they pulled us out of it; each of us readily admitted that these boys had saved us. We would have followed them to the end of the earth. Their parents we treated as royalty. We were so thankful for them having brought these beautiful guardian angels into the world that we bought them hot pretzels and coffees. We made them macramé and quilts and gave them badges with their son's photos on them; we bought their gas, gave them the motel rooms with river views when we went down on a long trip to West Virginia.

At 18-0 that February, the Marauders were unstoppable. Certainly they'd had good years before. Walter Haskins, who was the press operator at the *Daily News*, had made a scrapbook of their history for us—clippings he'd dug out of the paper's archives. He showed it around sometimes at games, in lulls in the play, or in someone's van on the road to an out-of-the-way tournament. The *Daily News* had always followed the Marauders because their coach, Sam Paris, was the sports editor there and had written all twenty-five years of Marauder history himself. And we enjoyed looking at the photos of these boys who were now men, reading about the limits of their accomplishments and failures. The more limited the past, we somehow reasoned, the more promising the future.

In retrospect, it is clear that our expectations might have been unfair, but to even speak of fairness is to miss the point. We needed them and they appeared—winners—riding a streak. No one doubted that we would walk into Akron in March and sweep the state tournament. There was talk of an AAU National Tournament berth, a trip to Atlanta.

And so when on this overcast February evening, we found ourselves in yet another insubstantial hamlet, and trailing at the beginning of the second period by eleven points to a group of kids who looked more like peasants from some forgotten epoch than a basketball team, we panicked.

Coach Sam Paris was a second-rate newspaperman, a practically incontrovertible fact. But he had a way of sapping every ounce of potential out of these boys. And this team's potential rivaled the best the town had ever seen. Their leading scorer, C.R. Conner, was actually thirteen and had to use a fake birth certificate, which we learned Haskins had created himself in the *Daily News'* pressroom. Already, *Street and Smith* had run a short piece about him, a potentially promising young college prospect. Once or twice, coaches from far-off cities to the north snooped around Marauder games, trying to get a look.

When C.R. scored, we whooped and hollered and carried on, physically incapable of not expressing our joy in wild gyrations and raised fists. Conner moved with real grace, slicing through opposing defenses for reverse lay-ups, turnaround jumpers. He had the instincts of someone twice his age and the other boys looked to him for leadership and inspiration, and he never let them down.

Except that night, in this town—there was some argument about whether it was called Riverton or Woodville—he faltered. He looked tired, like he hadn't slept, and we—shamefully; there are no excuses to be offered now—we suggested a number of unjust possibilities for this, among them drugs, a pregnant girlfriend, more failed classes.

We were at the height of our powers then. People at work or at the mall in Sugarton seemed to notice the new confidence, and sometimes even said as much. We felt invincible. We enjoyed bowling a few games and we all had personal bests that year. But we grew boisterous and arrogant, ridiculing folks on other lanes, calling back to the bar to have our beers brought to us. We talked loudly and wore loud clothes, funny hats. And we drank enormous amounts, thinking perhaps that if we pretended to be nineteen again, some physical change might in fact occur. It did not. And being asked by the management to not return did not even dent our mania.

We were unprepared for the Marauders to be down, though; it knocked the wind from us. This game was meant to be a mere warm-up for an upcoming tournament in Kentucky. We'd been using our energy reading Fodor's, booking rooms in Huntington, planning side trips to some local caverns and restaurants. This—this—was a practice, really. No more. Neither Riverton nor Woodville was even on any of our maps.

At first, we cheered louder. We tongue-lashed the referees. But these boys in their ancient Converse sneakers—again, there is dispute about what they were called, whether the Rockets, or the Green Dragons; someone thought the Flying Tigers—they had come to play, and they were capitalizing wholesale on the Marauders tentativeness. It didn't make any sense; these boys were almost effortlessly crushing the

Marauders. We searched for explanations, began to question Coach Paris' play-calling. Gradually we grew apoplectic.

Paris called time-outs and we could hear him berating the boys, the scuff of chalk on chalkboard, the seething breath forced between his teeth. The quiet in between his barks was deafening. He looked around the huddle and his gaze fell on Conner, who looked back at him with bewilderment in his eyes. The rest gasped for air like men emerged from the depths.

Mrs. Hollins announced to the rest of us that she could not watch this. She went to her car where, she later admitted, she found a distant university's classical radio station to which she could ride out the loss. She said she thought about the garden she would plant that spring, creating vast mental lists of all that she would put in it, the variations of potatoes and beans and squash, and all the ways she would care for those things.

Inside, we ate candy bars and drank flat soda. Some of us prayed, but the lead grew inordinately. Our boys played too cautiously; hesitant. They seemed such children just then.

Paris' assistant, Michael Watson, a sixth-grade science teacher at Hilltop Elementary, talked to Paris, entreated him. He would observe the court and then scribble on the chalkboard and try to show it to Paris, but Paris would look away, inconsolable.

Paris himself had been the sixth-man on Moraine High's only championship team of the last thirty years, and a few of us remembered him as the unskilled kid who came in to make life miserable for an opposing guard. Some said he was prone to starting fights; others believed the coach of that time had put him up to many of those fights, had sicced him on an opposing star in order to get them both ejected.

Though many of us had looked judgmentally upon his writing for years, we had all gained a great deal of respect for him as a coach, and when Carla Randolph began to assert that this was his fault—and many of us tried on that idea, of course—one of the true followers—it may have been Graham Wilson himself, who had fought off the Germans one yard at a time at the Bulge, turned to a group of us and said, "Just look at y'all. Y'all make me ashamed to be a Marauder." He was right. We were ashamed, too.

At half-time with the Marauders down by twenty-four, some of us went to look for a bar in the village—just a little shot in the arm to bolster ourselves. On our way out, we passed the cafeteria kitchen that the Marauders were using as a locker room. The door stood ajar and we could see Paris in the face of C.R. Conner, spit spraying as he tore into him. The other boys—Chad Holt, Nate Holland, and the others—sat impassively beyond them, exchanging water bottles, some with their hands splayed on bowed heads like young men who had just lost wives in a natural disaster.

Dim and dusty neon signs offered Bud and Miller Lite through the single, television-sized window outside the Raccoon Creek Tavern. It was bitter cold, well below zero, and we gingerly stepped across the frozen sand parking lot, interminable flurries flying all around us. Four trucks parked there sported provocative bumper stickers. It was not Cooley's, but we needed direly to regroup. Inside, the locals leered at us from their barstools. A few of them played pinball on dirty machines old enough to have been the first prototypes.

As we sipped at our drinks, Turner Olson suggested that perhaps they had fixed the game. Impossible, we said. We speculated on such other theories as the full moon and the re-emergence of Paris' ex-wife in Falls the week prior. But we couldn't get our finger on the situation. None of it added up.

We ordered a second round. Someone said we should be getting back and we all agreed, but none us made a move toward the door. Terry

Winston started to tell stories about his days as a Marauder, twenty years back.

"Paris was tough," he said. "A mean streak a mile long." His eyes lit up as he tried to retrieve that past so far behind him. He talked of a time when his knees were good, and of a game he once scored twenty-one points in. We listened like second-graders. He told tale after tale, about this or that boy—we knew all of them—and about Paris. One anecdote involved Paris, a boy named Chuck Wolf, and a full water bottle Paris had thrown across a gymnasium at the boy.

"It flew," Winston said, "right over his head and through one of the stained glass windows of this Catholic school's gym over in Chillicothe."

We all laughed at the image of Paris throwing a bottle at this boy, and then fell quiet as our laughs trailed off. Terry Winston shook his head.

"He'd scream bloody murder at us," he said. "Every minute of every game. He threatened us and insulted our manhood." He looked at each face there at the table.

"We never won a game," he admitted. "We did not win one game. Not ever." Mindy Hagan put her arm around him. He lowered his head and raised it again.

"But he would come into the locker room afterward and he would tell us how proud he was of us, and that he thanked God for us."

Winston looked to be on the verge of tears when Tad Phillips thought to order a bratwurst from the rotisserie from behind the bar, and salvaged the moment. None of us had eaten yet and so we all ordered bratwursts and more beers and listened to the general clatter as these things were delivered. Every one of us must have had a moment of clarity then as to what sort of people we were. We were not what any of us wanted to be. Eventually, it sunk in that we could not show our faces back at the gym.

Some hours later, we passed the aging elementary school on our way out of town. One dim yellow security bulb burned at a lonesome corner over the void of its parking lot. We drove in silence as we slipped back into the forests of that country, the winding roads, the nothing of that place. We checked our Rand McNally for the way home, and after several wrong turns and desolate stretches of emptiness, made our way back into Moraine County and then into Moraine proper. It was two in the morning then, and we drove past Cooley's to find it dark and closed, and we were all thankful not to face the choice of going in. We went home to the quiet lives we'd hoped we'd escaped. Those lives, of course, still awaited us, just as we'd left them months before, and we all felt them slip back toward us that night as we lay awake and waited for dawn.

Many of us were at Cooley's, hiding in coves in the back and eating fish sandwiches when the Saturday paper came out the next afternoon and confirmed the rumor circulating around town all morning—that the Marauders had pulled out a miracle, a come-from-behind victory.

We sat wordless and ashamed. A few tried to dig up the old enthusiasm, saying that the folks down in Kentucky better get ready, that the Marauders were going to storm the place. But no one really had the heart for it. We sat quietly in long stretches.

And then a curious thing happened: Graham Wilson walked in with a small entourage behind him, men and women we'd known our whole lives but who just then seemed unrecognizable, as foreign as a carload of Ukranians walking into that bar.

Wilson walked with a wiry old cherry cane that seemed a perfect symbol of his own dogged perseverance. When they'd settled in some booths upfront, he left his group and came over to ours. Wilson was decades older than any of us and we all knew he understood things that we did not. He approached our table and looked at us for a long minute without saying anything. He breathed heavily and pulled the unlit cigar from his mouth. We waited, preparing to take on the truth of his words, the rebuke we knew we deserved.

What we expected didn't come, though. "I reckon them boys we played last night took it hard. I near felt bad for 'em," he said, shaking his head.

He looked around the room like there might be a clue elsewhere in the smoky place for what to say to us. He might have said, "You people are pathetic," and he would have been right. But he didn't. What he said was much harder to take. He said, "We'll need you all down in Ken-tuck next week. We'll need ever last one of youns." And then he limped over to the bar and ordered a brandy and a Genesee like he always did.

We sat without words and fought within ourselves and finally we slid from our seats and paid our tabs and said quiet good-byes. And then every one of us walked through the oak door that led to the world outside. We pulled up our collars and put on our mittens and hats, and we bolstered ourselves against that winter afternoon as we walked right into it, some of us in silence, some of us mumbling to ourselves, and more than a few of us with clenched fists and voices crying out—part request, part demand—to the town of Moraine, or to the heavens, or to some unnamable thing inside. Indecipherable, guttural noises, grunts of the inarticulate, a triumphal sound from that part of us which knew how to answer Graham Wilson's demand.

Atlas

THE HIPPIES—there seems to have been universal agreement among the community on the appropriateness of this term, though I believe they identified themselves as the Fifth Regiment Peace and Justice Brigade, or something close to that—to the consternation of the municipality of Atlas, Ohio, had been camped out in Atlas Gardens Park much of that late summer and early fall. Nobody seemed to know why they'd decided on that spot nor, more importantly, how to get rid of them.

My cousin Phillip had specific orders not to go anywhere near the hippies. I'd gotten the same orders myself, both from my dad and from Uncle Donald. "Those dirty bastards are on drugs," Uncle Donald had told me—specifically me—again that morning. He was sitting in his recliner in threadbare underwear. "All you know, they're sacrificing kids down there." He likely believed this. Uncle Donald Dante's mind was a unique land populated by all manner of improbable scenarios about the world.

The police had already physically removed them once, but the action had been a public-relations disaster, because someone from the Columbus free paper had been on hand (one of the hippies, most likely) and portrayed the police action as unnecessarily violent. Which would've been par for the course, as far as the Columbus free paper was concerned, but there had been a recent police brutality episode in New York, and the bit about the Ohio hippies got mentioned in a paper there, and soon news crews were poking around southern Ohio. Did we have a police brutality epidemic on our hands? they wondered. This was exactly the sort of battle the town of Atlas was not prepared to fight. The hippies seemed to know this intuitively and a day or two later, they were back, just in time to make a national news program about police brutality, which I watched on the old cabinet TV downstairs because Dad didn't want to see it.

It was more or less impossible during that time to avoid the topic at Aunt Velma and Uncle Donald's; they lived, as I'd heard Uncle Donald say countless times, no more than a quarter-mile from the park.

My parents, though especially my dad, were loath to agree with Uncle Donald about anything, but the hippie business was impossible to see another way. Uncle Donald reveled in the rare alignment of the stars that brought he and my father into agreement and he trotted the topic out at every lull in the conversation.

Dad's chief concern, which I'd heard him go over three or four times with Uncle Donald, was that the hippies were defecating near the Highland River—he actually used that word, which was a piece of unusually technical diction for him. The Highland River brought drinking water to Moraine, twenty miles downstream, and you could see that the thought of getting sick from hippie e-coli was something my dad seemed to imagine in great detail and with extreme repulsion.

He had other concerns, too, mostly about the hippies sucking up welfare resources: free medical help, food stamps, government cheese. I knew he also objected to their preying on the good will of Catholic kitchens, which was not a point he chose to raise around Uncle Donald because, of all the things he didn't want to talk with Uncle Donald about, religion was primary.

Uncle Donald had an ax to grind with Catholicism, which, as a non-practicing but still-believing Catholic, made my dad uncomfortable. Like other aspects of Uncle Donald's character, this one just didn't make much sense; as far as I knew, he himself espoused no particular brand of religion, Christianity or otherwise. So any source of origin for the antipathy was possible—neo-Nazi propaganda at the bolt factory, anti-Kennedy sentiment from twenty years back; it was impossible to say. My suspicion was that it had to do with Notre Dame football.

In any case, Notre Dame generally seemed to elicit it. In fact, not an hour before the business with the hippies, Uncle Donald had again been railing against Catholicism (idolatry was today's theme) for the benefit of me and my brother Donnie, who was named after our paternal grandfather, not Uncle Donald. "Bad luck," I'd overheard my dad tell his own brother once, "Velma's husband having Dad's name."

Uncle Donald had been drinking steadily through the first half of a Notre Dame-Michigan match up in Ann Arbor. He was making quite a show of yahooing Michigan first downs and screaming obscenities at the Notre Dame players—"faggot" described everything from Notre Dame's Heisman-candidate flanker to the double reverse that scored them their first touchdown of the afternoon, as in, "that was a faggot play."

My dad did not approve of Uncle Donald's language. And no doubt understanding the subtext of the anti-Notre Dame rhetoric, he slipped out of the living room and into the kitchen to join the conversation going on between my mom and her sister.

Uncle Donald tried to act like he didn't care. "Tell you something, Junior," he said to me, leaning forward. He lowered his voice and looked toward the kitchen—something adolescent about that look. "Those faggot Irish aren't worth two shits." The Irish were in fact winning by seventeen. "You see if they all don't go to hell in the end, those god-damn idols around their necks."

Donnie cracked up at this. He thought Uncle Donald was hilarious. The idea that wearing crucifixes would send anyone to hell was just plain funny to me and Donnie because the mild-mannered Methodist church my mom sent us to would never dare cast aspersions on another sect. To say nothing of the fact that neither of us believed in much of it anyway.

Uncle Donald slugged the remainder of the beer in his hand, number four it appeared from a quick count of his empties, and he looked at Donnie. "Laugh, you little bugger," he said. "Just don't call me when Beelzebub is sticking you in the ass with his poker."

Donnie was, as a rule, not even in evidence during these visits. He preferred to hole up in Phillip's bedroom, reading *Shootout at Casa Grande* or the like, or to wander the neighborhood looking for cats to harass. But Uncle Donald after a few beers was something Donnie didn't like to miss and that alone was why he was still hanging around. He enjoyed the Beelzebub business.

"Why's he wanna stick me in the ass?" Donnie said to me. "Is Beelzebub a faggot?" And then the laughter started—small at first, just a giggle, but it gradually morphed into a cackle and then a full-body shake. After a short time, it began to infect me. Uncle Donald watched us with a smirk on his face, a strange and ignorant pride at somehow being the source of this. Soon the racket brought my mother into the room.

"What's the matter with you?" she asked Donnie. "Do you not have any sense?" Donnie was already beyond marshaling an answer; he looked like he was having trouble breathing, he was laughing so hard. When she looked at me, I knew to suppress my own laughter and shrug.

"Better check his drawers," Uncle Donald observed. "Probably crapped hisself." pants."

Then my mom sent Donnie to Phillip's room. Phillip, who was a year younger than Donnie and three older than me, was at football practice. It was a shame, too, because he usually took us to his friend Fisk's house and we'd light off fireworks or play video games. In three or four visits there, I'd never seen an adult.

When Mom returned to the kitchen, Uncle Donald looked at me and winked, as if he and I had just succeeded in yet another gag together. We could hear Donnie in there for some time cackling.

Aunt Velma came into the living room during the third quarter and handed Uncle Donald a scrap of paper and told him to take me to Kroger's to get some provisions for the picnic later that afternoon. Dad appeared behind her and unwittingly got roped into the mission as well. Only Donnie was safe, back in Phillip's bedroom, ensconced in his 1878 world of outlaws.

After Uncle Donald put some pants on, the three of us piled into his '73 Malibu, which was rusty on the quarter panels from winter salt, but otherwise clean and waxed. I sat in the spacious back, while Dad, up in the passenger seat, fastened his waist seatbelt, a move that Uncle Donald eyed suspiciously. This was before it became law to wear a seatbelt and I'd never seen Dad do it before, but before he had to turn around and tell me, I did the same.

Both Uncle Donald and Dad lit one of Uncle Donald's Winstons, and then Uncle Donald put the car in reverse and backed out of the small driveway. Theirs was one of those Levitt and Sons sort of postwar jobs; the entire block looked like a 1946 Uhaul advertisement, every house and concrete drive the same postage stamp dimensions, though all of it badly weathered by the intervening years.

The most unsettling thing about Uncle Donald was actually not the absurdity of his behavior but how normal it was in his neighborhood. His neighbor Chuck was out washing his car—an obsessive activity among men on the block—and so we idled in front of his house for a few minutes while the two of them chit-chatted, mostly about the rumor that Atlas Bolt Incorporated was on the bidding block. Chuck worked the nightshift there.

"Who you got in there?" Chuck wanted to know.

"Art here is married to Velma's sister. His boy's Nate."

It surprised me to hear Uncle Donald use my name. I wasn't sure he actually knew it.

"Ah," he said. "Folks from down Moraine."

"That's right," Dad said.

"I don't know if you've heard," he told Dad, squatting down so he could see him better. "But we've got a vermin problem in Atlas."

Dad acted like he didn't know what he was talking about. "Yeah?"

"Hippies," the guy belted out. "About forty or fifty hippies are camped out in our goddamn park."

"That," Dad said.

Chuck then shifted his weight so he could see me. "Stay away from those cocksuckers," he told me.

Even though the word was in common currency at school, it was embarrassing to have to hear it in front of my dad. But I nodded.

"We should go so we can get back," Dad said.

"That's right," Uncle Donald agreed, puffing profoundly on his cigarette and then giving Chuck a salute and putting the car into gear to drive on down Folgers Street, then Meridian, and then along Moraine.

Atlas Gardens Park was spread out along Moraine Street for over a mile. On the opposite side of the park was the river and on the other side of the river was the industrial wasteland where Atlas Bolt and a half-dozen other factories sat.

As we turned left onto Moraine, the hippies came into view immediately. It was like coming across a pack of javelinas in the desert: something different about the landscape invading your consciousness before you're quite aware of what it is. They were lying around in the early-afternoon sun, eating their granola or whatever. Some of them sat in circles with guitars and drums. They had an open fire over which a pot hung from a spit; many of them moved about industriously, cleaning up or preparing food. Scanning their faces, I recognized easily the one among them that didn't belong. He was wearing his thigh-pad girdle and his half-cut Atlas Summer Football Camp T-shirt, as if those two things alone were all that were necessary for a kid to wear for the sake of decency. Those girdles were made of mesh and you could see right through to the underwear. He was sitting on a large Guatemalan blanket, smoking a pipe.

Uncle Donald was murmuring under his breath as he drove along Moraine Street. It wasn't uncommon for him to go on in the manner of Popeye about nothing in particular; during Ohio State games, he let out an almost constant unconscious stream of self-talk.

"You believe this, Art?" he asked my dad now, opening up the topic for the fourth time today. Dad, who had been actively avoiding looking toward the park, reluctantly moved his gaze in that direction. He nodded.

I watched him to see if he had spotted Phillip. Something in the stiffness of his shoulders told me that he had. But he obviously had no intention of pointing this out to Uncle Donald. I thought I had some idea of what would happen if he saw Phillip. I'd not seen a full-fledged version of Donald's meanness at that point, but even the short unhappy dinner table exchanges I *had* seen foretold of his terrible potential.

For the moment, Uncle Donald was deep into a diatribe against the kids who had gone to Canada during the last war; he himself had come of age while shooting at Japanese boys at Guadalcanal, which to hear him tell was an experience everyone should have. In his opinion, he was saying, these draft dodgers should be hunted down and shot the way they would've been by the Soviets, whose tactics he frequently extolled.

In the midst of a stream of unrelenting vitriol along these lines—he could move seamlessly, and in the same breath, from Carter to Canada to the EPA and finally to the hippies—he took one more look across the field, just to fill himself with the disgust he liked to be filled with. He was shaking his head, clearly enjoying the scene in his way. And then, without any sound at all, without slowing down, he turned the car toward the park gently, as if it were a schooner, and drove right over the four-inch curb, never dropping below thirty miles per hour. Uncle Donald, who had no seatbelt on, hit his head on the roof. He cut through the middle of the park toward the place where Phillip sat. The hippies, who were accustomed to all sorts of hostility, recognized the unfolding action immediately and scattered like grasshoppers.

Uncle Donald skidded to a stop across the grass not ten feet from Phillip, who must've been too stoned to run, or care. Uncle Donald looked around the car then—on the floor, in the back seat, even in the glove box—for something, apparently, to beat his son with. Finding nothing, he decided to go ahead without a tool. He got out and left the door open and strode toward Phillip.

Phillip took a quick glance at us and then looked back toward his approaching father and said, "Dad, no." But he knew better. Or should have. He'd lived his whole life with Donald Dante; the single-mindedness of his father's vision of the world was as big a truth for Phillip as the rising of the sun. Uncle Donald struck him four times in the head with his fist. My dad and I watched with horror for a long moment and then Dad opened his door and lifted his head and said, "That's enough, Donald." Donald hit him one more time, and then stopped, panting. Phillip was in a pile on the blanket. A few of the hippies had returned, apparently seeing that they themselves were in no danger.

"That's child abuse," a young woman said. "That's fucking child abuse."

Uncle Donald was in some other world, though. "Huh?" he said, only vaguely aware of the direction of the voice.

"You heard me, you pig," she said. "This isn't the dark ages. You can't beat your children like that."

"You can't beat your children like that," he mocked in an absurdly high voice.

A couple other girls had gone over to see if Phillip was alright. He shook them away, though. He was crying, but was getting up anyway. He picked up his pants and pads and helmet and eventually came around to the back door and threw them in next to me and got in.

"Mind your own business, sweetheart," Donald said, regaining his composure. "Go plant a goddamn tree."

"This is my business," she said. "Human life is all my business. It's my *only* business."

"Come on, Donald," my dad said now.

My dad had probably noticed the gradual return of the rest of the hippies, some of the men appearing above the bluffs, looking like former football players themselves.

Donald turned to look to my dad. "Goddamn sixties ruined everything," he said. Nobody said anything more, though—not to him. One of the girls—a pretty young woman whose breasts were clearly visible through a thin T-shirt—came over to my side of the car—Phillip's window was rolled up—and reached across me and extended a brown-eyed Susan toward Phillip. He was looking straight ahead. "It'll be okay, Phillip," she told him.

Phillip didn't look at her or take the flower. "Fuck your fucking fucking flower," he spat. That might have been enough to elicit a slap from my own dad normally, but he neither did nor said anything. Uncle Donald got back in then and slammed his door. The girl stepped away.

He sat there for a moment. The rage in him was not yet extinguished. There were maybe seven or eight hippies near the car, looking at us. Dad was trying to be patient, seemed to be staring at a willow in the distance. Then Donald turned and grabbed a fistful of my T-shirt. "Get yourself an eyeful, Nate. Remember this. This is what you don't want to be. This boy is showing you how *not* to live."

I just looked at him and quietly, almost imperceptibly, nodded. My dad put his hand on Uncle Donald's arm then and Donald let go of me, turned, put the car in reverse and drove back to the street.

At the store, Dad told me to go in with Uncle Donald. At first, it seemed a strange decision, but I realized that he probably wanted to talk to Phillip.

So Uncle Donald and I silently picked out buns and hot dogs and beer and ketchup and some other things and threw them into a noisy-wheeled cart. There was more self-talk, but nothing addressed to me. Uncle Donald paid for the items with an unorganized wad of bills—bar cash leftovers. When we returned, Phillip lay curled up, sleeping off his high. Dad sat silent and distant.

The trip back to the house, too, passed without sound. When we pulled into the driveway, Phillip and I headed up the front stairs, but as I was opening the door, I heard Dad ask Uncle Donald to wait for a minute. Phillip went on toward his room, but I lingered inside the door. From there, I could see Dad and Uncle Donald through a gap in the shade covering the small diamond-shaped window.

The conversation was short. Dad came around the car and stood quite close to Uncle Donald. Uncle Donald did his best to suggest that he was not afraid of my dad, but his body language gave him away.

"Donald, I realize Phillip is your boy," Dad said. "But I don't want to see or even hear of you ever laying a hand on him again."

"You got your style and I got mine, Art," Uncle Donald said.

"I'll not have an argument with you about it," Dad said. Their voices came through the aluminum siding clear enough. "Just don't ever do it again."

Dad started to walk toward the door then and I ran on through the living room toward Phillip's room. His door was opened and he was already sitting on the floor. Donnie lay on the bed, his book face down in front of him.

"The fuck you do?" Donnie asked him. As someone who had seen his share of trouble, Donnie could smell it in the air. I stepped into the room, out of my Dad's line of sight.

"You were down to the park," Donnie said.

Philip nodded.

"Hangin' out with Astral and the gang."

Of course Donnie knew them. Philip wasn't even surprised. Neither was I.

"You boys leave Phillip alone," Dad said now from behind me. "Go out to the yard and find something to do there." He didn't need to say, "Don't leave the yard."

Donnie and I shuffled past Dad and then he closed Philip's door. Outside, I told Donnie what had happened. He listened patiently, interrupting a few times to say things like, "Then what did Dad say?" Or, "Right through the fucking park?"

When I was done with the story, he nodded. "Man, if he's not careful, Dad's going to knock his dick in the dirt." He laughed at the thought of it and added, "I for one wouldn't mind seeing it."

Uncle Donald himself appeared then on the small stoop at the back door. He looked out at us as if he were surveying a vast prairie. Their yard was not much bigger than the average garage. It had a table with an umbrella and three ratty chairs in the middle. Otherwise, one sickly oak tree grew in the corner, and Donnie sat in one of its low branches. I leaned on a sagging red fence that separated their yard from the Culpepper's grilling area.

It was clear enough that he had come outside to cool down. He sat at the table and ignored us, opening a new pack of cigarettes, tapping one out and lighting it. He smoked quietly through that first one. Me and Donnie watched him and looked at each other. At one point my Dad appeared in the window long enough to see where we were and where Uncle Donald was.

"You boys have no idea," Uncle Donald said, perhaps feeling that presence.

"About what?" Donnie said.

"You know God damn and well about what. The world didn't used to be like this."

"What was it like?" Donnie asked. His voice was thick with sarcasm. He was not afraid of Uncle Donald and as he came into adolescence, he was increasingly testing Uncle Donald's limits and powers—he knew better than to try this sort of thing with Mom or Dad.

Uncle Donald decided not to address himself to Donnie anymore.

"You didn't used to have to put up with that bullshit, Nate," he said.

"Now you do," Donnie said. "Now even the hippies have equal rights, don't they?"

"Your old man can't tell me how to raise my kids." Still, he was looking at me. This was dangerous territory. There was something troubling about seeing Uncle Donald so upset, because though he bitched a lot, he didn't have any real gripes with life. The bitching was just what he did, who he was. "It's just not the way it works," he said.

"Maybe you shouldn't beat your son," Donnie said.

"I'll decide what I should and shouldn't do."

"Seems like maybe you won't."

Uncle Donald looked at Donnie, obviously thinking better of going after him. He picked up his cigarette package and lighter and got up to go inside.

"It's a whole new world," Donnie told Uncle Donald as he went.

Donnie was not mean as a rule; Uncle Donald just brought something out in him, some streak of irreverence. But these words suggested a deeper knowledge of the world than he could possibly have had. At fifteen, Donnie didn't know anything about the way the world had been or in what ways it was changing. He knew only that Uncle Donald would be most disturbed by these words. You had to watch television with Uncle Donald only a few times to understand that his deepest fear was that the world was changing and for the worse.

After Uncle Donald had gone inside, I said, "You're making things worse for Philip."

"You're a punk," he said, turning on me. He swung on a branch and landed in the yard. "Philip knows what he needs to do."

At the park, we sweated under the sun and ate our hot dogs and macaroni salad, marched through the routine of the family picnic. Nobody mentioned the fact that a half-mile upriver the hippies were having their own Saturday afternoon festivities. Nobody needed to.

Toward nightfall, Philip and Uncle Donald, now a team, started to run the horseshoe pit. Uncle Donald was by then good and drunk, plowed, really, and had forgiven his son. Likely forgotten everything. The whole party had relocated to watch.

With the group congregated close together like that, I noticed my dad was missing. I scanned the crowd, waited for him to return from the bathroom. His absence was particularly conspicuous because usually he was involved in any horseshoe action.

As if from thin air, my brother appeared at my side then. Actually, slightly behind me, that knowing whisperer in my ear he sometimes was. "Who you looking for?"

"No one. You're strange."

"I know," he said, and then: "He's down with the hippies."

"Who's down with the hippies?"

"Come on, now."

"How do you know?"

I knew exactly how he knew. He knew I knew exactly how he knew. He smiled that infuriating smile of risk and knowledge. As if on cue, Dad emerged from the trail that ran along the bluffs up and down the park. Donnie winked.

"Probably smokin' himself some ganja," he said.

I just looked at him blankly. I was hoping, I think, that the difference between us was more than just four years. But he seemed to see into me then; it was another of his skills, knowing when I'd had enough.

"I'm just messin' with you, hoss," he said. "You know that, right?"

"Yeah, Donnie," I said. "I know."

"Crazy shit today, huh? Nothing but par for the course, though. People do crazy shit all the time. That's what I've learned."

I watched Phillip hit a ringer to end the game with two of Mom's brothers.

"Dad ain't going to be smoking no weed," he said, observing Dad coming toward us then. "He was just talking to them. That's all."

What could my dad possibly have said to the hippies? I wondered. Don't shit near the river? I thought about just asking him, but then thought better of it. Surely he didn't attempt to explain to them why they should move on. But maybe he didn't talk to them all; it wasn't above Donnie to fabricate the whole mess. He enjoyed intrigue. My problem was that my ignorance was big enough already without these galling mysteries.

Dad approached the crowd, smoking a cigarette. He saw the show going on in the horseshoe pit—Phillip and Uncle Donald were celebrating now with a victory do-si-do, Uncle Donald himself providing the hillbilly soundtrack—and I could see in his face a frustration with the way the world sometimes was, how it did not act as it should. I wanted to reassure him, because I knew that that frustration had to do with me somehow, with what I'd seen. But he was, finally, remote, unapproachable. For all of the will of his heart, he and I were finally two different species. So I stood where I was, Donnie already disappeared, dusk's dark confusion deepening the shade of the giant maples. The crowd, distant family, second cousins, great aunts, clapped along with Uncle Donald's song, as oblivious to the rotten core of the moment as fishes of land.

Slump

BROOKWATER'S FIRST ERROR was impossible to forget. It came in the bottom of the seventh against Kentucky Fried Chicken—and they only *had* seven innings at this level. With the score at 3-4, and Rotary winning, KFC, the visiting team, had one last go at it. They had base-runners on second and third and the top of their order at the plate.

With a 2-2 count, the pitcher—a boy named González—threw a fastball strike, a meaty pitch, and the ball came off the bat with a piercing crack. He had gotten all there was to get of it, and it went straight up the middle, nearly taking out the pitcher, scudding hard overtop second base.

It surprised no one when the diving body of Sherman Brookwater disappeared into a cloud of dust behind second base and an instant later sprung upright with the ball transferring from glove to right hand. In nearly one motion, he looked back at the base runner on third, and then took the step toward first to make the out, the boy who had hit the ball not even halfway to first.

But then something happened. Brookwater released the ball too late, and it flew past the first basemen wide to the left—fifteen, maybe twenty feet wide. A very long moment of disbelief fell among those watching, a real quiet spreading over the place. And then it became a foot race.

Rotary's first baseman, a kid easily thirty pounds overweight, turned to where the ball had gone and threw down his glove and started out after it; if Brookwater had run after it himself, he might have gotten there sooner. The base runner on third scored easily to tie the game, and the one on second came rounding third for home, his coach jumping up and down, swinging his arm in mad circles like some human haywire timepiece.

Through all of this, Brookwater stood where he had just seconds before made the errant toss. You could see it drain from him, whatever it was that had made him stand out. He watched as the first baseman finally reached the ball and turned to throw it home. He stood, impassive, holding his glove strangely at his side; it seemed not to contain a hand at all anymore, but some maimed limb.

The throw to home was a good one and precipitated another cloud of dust, larger than the one that had begun the play behind second, but it didn't even need to settle for Stewart Johnson, the behind-the-plate umpire, to make the call, because the ball had trickled out of the catcher's glove and it rolled right up against Stewart's foot.

"Safe," Stewart called, spreading his arms wide to his sides.

The troubling thing was how easily and quickly the memory of that play dissipated in everyone's minds, supplanted by the other one, the Brookwater throw.

Brookwater walked off the field and went to the dugout where the second-string sat. Soon the other fielders made their way in and sat as well, but all of them seemed to avoid getting too near Brookwater. He was not a big boy, not intimidating. This distance came more from respect than fear.

The coach said very little to the team. "We got General Electric on Tuesday," was really *all* he said, and the boys dispersed sullenly.

Brookwater walked to the parking lot where his parents and his little brother were waiting in their truck, and then he climbed into the cab and his father drove them away. Soon the parking lot was nearly vacant, and as those cars emptied out onto Second Street, you couldn't mistake the feeling in the air. It seemed that no one felt quite right about what had happened, not even the boys on KFC, who had improved their record to 7-3 and moved into a tie for second place.

I was the second-base umpire that night, as I was most nights in those years. I remember that I stood next to the backstop afterward and exchanged but a few words with Stewart Johnson, both of us, I think, a little dumbfounded by what had transpired. We didn't speak of it, though. We just looked at each other, our eyes big with surprise. We shook our heads. Stewart's wife pulled their El Camino into the lot. "See you tomorrow," he said finally. "Yep," I said.

He threw his chest protector into the bed and got inside and they pulled away. I leaned back against the mesh fence of the backstop then. The city park was nearly empty, all of those people going home to have dinner and watch television and talk about their days. I knew that at any moment I could go home myself—kiss my wife Helen, play with my daughter Jessica. I could take a cool shower and put on some shorts and maybe read for a while. There were plenty of things I could do or not do. I could go to sleep after midnight and wake late, because it was June, and school was out.

But for a long time I stood there, leaning against the backstop and looking out into the darkness coming on. I think I saw my life for a moment there without the blurring vision of someone living it, but from—not exactly outside it, but not completely in it, either. I saw, somehow, how my life had unfolded, how I had ended up here and not somewhere else. I was still young, still close enough to the beginning to remember what some of the other paths might have been, but far enough down one of those paths to not be able to turn back in any significant way, and it seemed strange to me for a moment to be the man I was. It just seemed weird, being alive, I guess. And then I began to remember my own failures, my own blundered throws and catches, things I should have said but didn't, things I shouldn't have said but did—a full, if mostly innocuous, chest of misadventures and shortcomings. In calling up all this, it occurred to me that I was just as much the person who had fallen down those times as the one who'd gotten back up afterward, and that I was not just the figure masquerading through my life as me, but these other people from along the way, too.

Inexplicably, the beginning of Sherman Brookwater's slump was what brought me to that. I felt a terrible sense of dread for him that night. Being around children everyday as I am at the school, it's easy to forget the weight of it all, that immense desire to make the right choices, to separate yourself out, to become someone. His first error seemed emblematic of something much greater than it should have. I had a feeling already, that first night, that it would prove to be more than just an isolated event, that it would carry weight of its own. And as I watched each of those errors unfold over the following weeks, I understood that feeling no better, but saw that it was true.

Out past centerfield was another field—the pony-league field—and then beyond that, in descending order, the three things that had linked Moraine with the rest of the world for 150 years—the highway, then the railroad tracks, and then the river. I hadn't ever thought of it quite like that, that if you wanted to get in or out of Moraine, that's always been the way, right down the center of the valley, northwest toward the city. Cars were shuttling by on US 33 then—the only of the three still in use—their lights coming on now against the fog creeping up the valley. I sat there a little longer, my mind drifting away from these things eventually, and when it was nearly dark, I walked to my truck and drove home.

Some summer-school flunkies saw Frank Brookwater down at the field with his two boys a lot that week. Apparently in the morning before work he'd roust the boys out of bed and take them down there and he'd put Sherman out at second base and his little brother Sheridan over at first. The sun would just be cresting the hills to the east of town and these summer-school boys—three of them, all part of the Hogben clan— would be walking by the field and they'd see the Brookwaters out there practicing, and they'd sit down and have a dip of Skoal and watch.

I saw these three boys one July day in the cafeteria—Wayne, Sutton, and Mike, the first two brothers, the latter, their cousin—and I sat with them.

The cafeteria ran a small a la carte line in the summer months, for the students and teachers who had the misfortune of working, and for the painters and carpenters who were habitually at work somewhere on the grounds. I liked to go up there and get a ham and cheese sandwich and a coffee, maybe a Swiss Roll, and talk to someone; I was generally by myself down in the shop, where I spent a lot of time in the summer because there was better equipment there than at my house. That summer I was building a Shaker bed for my wife's birthday.

"Uh oh," Mike said as I sat my plate down.

"Boys," I said.

"Hey, Mr. Kern."

"What's new?" I asked.

"Nothing," Wayne said. And then his brother Sutton groaned. "Why you have to sit with us, man? The whole place is practically empty. We're not doing nothing' wrong."

The other two laughed.

"Because," I said. "I want to know what's going on in your lives, how summer school is going. I'm not here to hassle you."

He groaned again, but quickly went back to eating his hamburger, and the four of us made small talk for some time. These kids were trouble. Their parents were no good—not as citizens, not as parents, not as anything. The boys would most almost certainly end up in the system in one way or another. At best, they would find work doing demolition on old buildings. At worst was a proposition I didn't even want to consider.

I didn't ask them about Brookwater; they were talking about him among themselves. They were laughing about the idea of a dad—particularly their own—getting his kids out of bed to go practice in the morning.

"You talking about Sherman Brookwater?" I asked, trying not to sound overly curious.

"I don't know," Sutton said. "Yeah, that's what the old man calls him. Sherman."

"*Sherman*," Wayne said derisively.

"He's got him practicing in the mornings, does he?"

"I guess that's what you'd call it," Mike said. "He yells at him and makes him run laps and stuff."

"And he hits big ole grounders at him," Wayne added. "Hard ones, like he's Reggie Jackson or something."

"Yesterday," Mike said, "he hit one so hard that it came up his arm and hit 'im in the face and give 'em a black eye."

"Yeah," Wayne added. "And just then, when that boy missed the ball, the old man goes over and leans against the fence like he's in pain, and then he says something like 'Go on an' git it'—like he's talking to someone on the other side of the fence. 'And do a lap.' Six-thirty in the morning, man. I'd like to see old Harlan Hogben say that to me."

They all laughed uncontrollably.

"Shoot," Sutton said finally. "And you can see his brother over there at first just lovin' it." They laughed again, and were still laughing when I got up and headed back toward the shop.

Rotary played that Tuesday against General Electric and that was when Sherman Brookwater's slump began in earnest. He threw away three easy outs and duffed two more meekly-hit grounders. Afterward he did not ride home with his family, but walked the mile and a half to his house. People saw him almost limping along Front Street, his head hanging low, his white uniform filthy; nobody knew if his dad had made him walk or if he had done it himself. I drove by him and offered him a ride, as I'm sure others had, but he never even looked up.

Once the slump began, it was on for good, and it didn't take long for it to reach a point of completeness, a point of thorough and unequivocal failure. It was not possible really to fail worse, and by the time this became clear, everyone seemed dismayed, and seemed to hope that every time a ball flew off a bat that it would go to Sherman and that he would make the play and look this thing in the eye, and beat it. But he never did.

During the afternoons of the slump that summer—this was late June and then all of July—I would see Sherman Brookwater at the library, because Helen worked there. He was always in some new corner of the place, reading about Greek city-states or the northern lights or some other exotic topic. I would casually glance at the title of the book in front of him from across the room. He sometimes checked things out, but mostly he read them right there, and all day long. He read Hamlin Garland and Charles Dickens and Isaac Asimov. Some days he would pull out the big Atlas and methodically go through all of the continents and countries and cities in the world, as if he were searching for one particular place—he worked with that sort of concentration, as if it were all just a search for a single location.

Sherman was an average student. "Middle of the class, maybe lower," a woman—his fifth-grade teacher?—once told a small group at a Rotary game. Many people spoke of this reading thing—a fact apparently generally known, though I had nothing to do with it—as if it were some sad manner of dealing with the slump. It seemed natural enough to me.

People saw him at the pool, too—and on game days, something widely known to be off-limits. But Sherman made a point of it, swimming some laps and then getting out and to go rest up against the fence and talk to his friends, as conspicuous as a lifeguard. "If you go to the pool on game day and so much as dip your foot into the water," Sherman's coach had warned earlier that season, "you won't even pinch-run for my team." But then Sherman went to the pool, out in the open, did triple springs on the board (also illegal) and high, careening dives, what the boys called "jays," so that the splash shot high into the air, as if from a whale's spout, drenching girls who were laying out or, if he hit a good one, drenching his friends on the other side of the fence.

His coach knew; there's no way he couldn't have. But the only change in Sherman's position in the line-up was to be moved to shortstop for two games, a move that had no net effect on his fielding slump. By that point, everyone suspected that it would never end, and that it was now part of who he was.

By the beginning of August, Sherman Brookwater was not really even playing much anymore. He would start the games, but his coach would substitute for him halfway through; it seemed only fair to give the second-string boys a chance. They couldn't, Sherman's coach reasonably argued, do any worse than Sherman Brookwater.

After those games, Sherman and his dad would walk away together, the father's arm over the boy's shoulder, tenderly guiding him toward the truck. His mother and brother would be walking with them, on the other side of Sherman, and Frank Brookwater would be speaking to

Sherman. You wondered what a man could say to a boy who had failed like that, and it made me respect Frank Brookwater a whole lot the way he seemed to have come around. The last thing Sherman needed, after all, was his father berating him. As it was, it seemed like Sherman and his family had made peace with his failure. I don't believe, however, the same can be said about many of us who had been watching it happen. It was such an odd case, to see a boy with that sort of promise and natural ability lose it all as if by magic. For years, you would hear people talk about it. We shook our heads a great deal that summer.

Finally, in early August, the season's last games—rain make-ups—were played. Rotary lost to the Shake Shoppe in their final game, 13-4, and ended the season with eight wins and twelve losses. They had once been 8-1. They did not come in last place, because Appalachian Oil had won only three games, but their failure seemed to transcend last place, to be something much worse than last.

One day, years later, I came to understand all of this.

The truth was—I believe—that Sherman Brookwater never had a slump. True, he made twenty-eight errors—never, in fact, truly made a play after the KFC game, not counting catching a few force outs at second. True, I saw every one of his errors happen and can verify for you that they did happen; I saw them with my better than twenty-twenty vision. But it was a supreme illusion. I believe that Sherman fabricated the slump. He faked it.

My daughter Jessica was a couple years younger than Sherman Brookwater and so through the years of Sherman's adolescence, I heard, from time to time, about his odd progress in life. I sat in the third row that very autumn in Moraine High School's auditorium for County History Day. I listened that afternoon to Sherman give a ten minute presentation on the German V2 Rockets and their use late in World War II, a presentation for which he was awarded a blue ribbon. I had never heard of any use of rockets in the war and thought for one strange moment that he might have made it all up and fooled everyone. The following Monday, though, I looked it up in the encyclopedia in our high school's library and saw that such rockets had indeed existed, very much the way Sherman had characterized them.

The spring following the summer of Sherman's slump, when sheets were passed around at school for baseball sign-up, Sherman did not, apparently, raise his hand for one. At the time, surely some of the other boys said something to him; it is impossible for me to know. To be fair, a lot of boys dropped out of baseball between sixth and seventh grade. Those who stayed had to jump up into the next league and face boys as old as sixteen. It was not entirely odd for a boy to gracefully bow out of the sport at that age, and though he was an exceptional example, people seemed to take it in stride, as an almost predictable thing: Sherman Brookwater had lost his confidence and he would never get it back, not in baseball at least. He was smart in a way to leave it behind, people said. Something like that could trail you around your whole life if you weren't careful.

By the summer before his freshman year, he was practically invisible—at least according to my daughter. That summer would have been his last, theoretically, in the city recreational league. To my knowledge, he never played another game at the city park after Rotary's last game there three years before; he had that night dropped a pop fly, duffed a grounder, and tripped over second base on an attempted double play, all in the first three innings; he had sat the rest of the game at the end of the bench.

During his freshman year, he was a student of mine for a semester. Among the two or three projects he made in that class, the best was a quite professional-looking metal ruler. During the time he was my student, we never spoke outside of class. The urge struck me more than once to ask him into my office, but I don't know what I might have said to him. If he remembered me, he never made any indication of it. In class, he would answer my questions as well as any of the other kids— questions about protective equipment and operating the lathe. Shop class is not a difficult business.

He did not seem a particularly sullen or insecure boy, which I guess surprised me some. I couldn't help but remember the kid who had become so accustomed to failure that he seemed to know it was about to happen; the two boys—the older and younger Shermans—seemed completely different people.

He got an A in my class. I checked his records on the computer and discovered that he got As in most of his classes. He had clearly grown to be a bright, industrious young man. He spent most of his Junior year as a Kiwanis exchange student in Guadeloupe, and I remember late that year seeing him standing in the hallway near the auditorium during lunch, talking in fluent French with Mrs. Holloway, our languages teacher. It intimidated me in some strange way that he could do that, that he could just walk away from this place and learn to make sounds that we could not understand. I felt some inexplicable confusion about that—almost an anger.

His senior year, just months before he left Moraine for a large university in Colorado, I had one more run-in with Sherman Brookwater. It was mid-spring, coming up on six years since the summer of his slump.

I had been asked by Steve Walters, one of our gym teachers, if I could cover his eighth period class; his son had a last minute doctor's appointment. In exchange, he would cover my first period the following Monday, and I could sleep in for fifty more minutes. It was a fine trade, the kind of thing that went on regularly among the two of us, and among many other teachers as well. They were playing softball, he told me. All I had to do was observe; the boys did the same thing everyday, and they knew what to do.

There were three games going on and I wandered among them as they played, not paying any real attention. There were probably sixty or seventy kids on the field, total. It had rained earlier in the day, and it was a little muggy for April, but nice, too. Good baseball weather, really.

I was standing in the middle of the three games when I recognized him, inhabiting his old spot at second base on field number two. I believe it was not his face that I recognized, but the way he paced around in between pitches, for I was a little too far off to see any of his features well. I casually shifted over toward the first base line of that game, next to the football field's visiting bleachers, and I leaned up against the structure and checked my watch. Time was short; by the time all the boys got dressed and onto the field, there was really only twenty-five minutes or so to play before they had to go back in and change. The class was the last of the day—the last of the week—and my wife and I were having dinner with some friends that night, and I was thinking about that as I stood there.

There were runners on first and third, Francis Brown and Nate Holland—boys I'd also known from my umpiring days—and the game's pace had picked up a little because the boys knew time was short, too, and, I gathered from their cheers, the team at bat was down by just a run or two.

The next batter was a lefty, thin and wiry-looking, whose name I don't think I ever knew. He swung hard at the first pitch and pulled a line drive just foul down the first base line. The ball hit the ground twice and then bounced up in what we used to call a candy hop and landed squarely in my hands. Some of the boys applauded my stop as I threw the ball back to the pitcher, and I feigned modesty, though I had been a strong third baseman in my day.

The next pitch was a slow, high-arcing thing that took forever to reach the batter, but when it finally did, the boy took another strong cut, and tore into the ball, sending another shot toward first base, this time on the fair side of the line. It was something between a line drive and a fly ball and it seemed that it would turn into a very nice single, or possibly even a double if he were a fast kid.

But then I saw the figure of Sherman Brookwater explode; he seemed to be doing something more than running, he moved so quickly. He was coming straight toward me, as the ball would soon be dropping very close to where I stood.

All of this passed much quicker than the time it will take to tell it.

I watched as Brookwater ran this ball down, somehow beating it to the spot. I could hear the exhalations of his breath and then, as he dove hard onto the damp playing field, I could hear the soft grunt he made when he landed. An instant later, he held the ball in his glove, his arm extended above his supine body. But the play was not over, and in the next instant, he sprung up and, in an adult version of the wonder I had witnessed those years before, turned and threw a perfect strike—across his body, off-balance, maybe thirty-five yards—to the third baseman, catching the base-runner who had not tagged up.

It was a double play—I had seen him make many of those once upon a time—and the throw ended the inning. But there was a moment afterward in which things moved much slower and in that time I heard boys shouting and the distant whistle of a girl's gym class and the sound of a ball hitting a bat in one of the other games. Also in that time, Sherman Brookwater turned and looked to me and told me the whole story with a single glance.

In that brief glance, Sherman Brookwater gave me to understand the mystery I had turned over in my mind those years, and I immediately began calling up the images of Sherman making the errors he had made—no one was closer than I for most them. I had seen them and with what I felt was good judgment. But never did I imagine what became clear to me then. As I replayed them in my mind—one by one they came back, as if they had been my own—I watched his eyes, his hands, his head, and I saw the discrepancy between what I'd seen and what I'd thought I'd seen; I was horrified.

He had made them on purpose. He had closed his eyes, turned his glove, tripped himself. It wasn't something I would ever be able to explain to another person. No one would believe it.

I stood there and I think I mouthed the word Jesus, but not *to* anyone; Sherman had already turned his back on me, and was jogging off the field. I turned toward the row of white pine that separated the school grounds from Hancock Street. I put my hands on my head and just closed my eyes for a minute.

"It's time to go in," said a boy next to me, holding up his arm for me to see his digital watch. "You need to blow the whistle."

I looked to the boy and then reached to my neck and took hold of the string and pulled the whistle over my head and I gave it to him. He looked at me, confused.

"You blow it," I said. "Would you?"

He continued to stare, as if he weren't quite sure who or what I was.

"Blow it, dammit," I said, not looking at him this time.

Then he did and I heard its piercing screech and the ensuing low rumble of the kids running across the turf.

It was as if it had all been for me, I thought. It felt like that—that Sherman Brookwater's elaborate vanishing act: the slump, but the gradual morphing into this other person, too—had been solely for me. I squeezed my fists white.

In the locker room, Sherman was seated, pulling on his shoes. The din of noise was monstrous, lockers slamming and the weight-room stereo tuned into a crackly hard rock station and random cheers and laughs and showers running. Nobody paid any attention to me when I walked in.

I approached him immediately. "You've got it all wrong," I told him. He didn't hear me, or pretended not to.

"Sherman," I said. He looked up from where he was tying a shoe.

"Huh?"

"It's wrong," I said.

Now he sat up, his shoes tied. "I'm sorry?"

"You can't just fake something like that," I said. "You can't just kill a part of yourself." But I knew as I said it that I was dead wrong.

He squinted at me, as if I were very small and he were simply trying to see me.

"I'm not sure what you're talking about, Mr. Kern," he said. He looked genuinely bewildered that I would be talking about killing things, and it seemed, somehow, that he had just wanted me to know—who knows why. Because he rightly suspected that it mattered to me. But he had nothing to gain by explaining it all now, six years after the fact, how he had sabotaged himself. Why.

He had done it, and it had changed his future as he knew it would. And now it seemed it was possibly going to change mine, too. In some small way, this was going to uproot how I thought about my life, though I don't think Sherman really meant for that to happen. It just did.

The bell rang and boys went running in all directions, and the last of the showers was finally turned off. Sherman stood up to leave and grabbed three books from the top shelf of his locker. He paused there for a moment, an act of courtesy. I wasn't looking at him anymore, though, but at the ground. I shook my head. "Have a good weekend, Sherman," I told him. "Forget about it."

"All right," he said. "Have a good weekend, Mr. Kern." And then I watched him walk around the corner, and when he disappeared through the door, something made me follow him. When I got to the door that led outside, I saw that he had already descended the stairs along the stadium and was walking on the track toward the locked gate along Mulberry Street, the place where trucks could enter the field if they needed to.

I walked along the top row of the stadium and leaned against its back wall and watched as he walked around the track, that unmistakable and graceful gait that had persisted through adolescence. When he got to the gate, he started to squeeze through the small opening where the chain locking the two bars together wasn't quite taut. He threw his books onto the concrete sidewalk on the other side, and then stuck his right foot through, and for a moment, he had his feet pointing in opposite directions, like the figures in Egyptian paintings. He turned his head to the side then, so that he could fit it through, and then slowly he moved it past the bars. Finally, he pulled his other leg through, and reached down and picked up his books, and began walking up Mulberry Street. And just as he was just about to disappear, I wasn't thinking about where he would be going. I was wondering how he had gotten through that damn gate.

Drowned Boy

1.

Afterward, the three girls left the gymnasium through the side doors into a night moonless and freezing, two degrees Fahrenheit. People from Moraine, Ohio, and the nearby hamlets of Tripoli and Falls smoked cigarettes and pipes and made their slow way toward trucks and cars parked on the winding, hilly streets surrounding the old and decrepit high school. The cold air was dense and voices issuing up and down the block carried no farther than arm's reach within it before dissipating into the ether of space and darkness.

The girls observed a silence of their own as they walked down along Market Street and then Midland Avenue. This could have had to do with the game, which Moraine had lost, or the boy's death, either one; Samantha didn't know for sure which.

She decided to leave the silence alone, in any case, and when they arrived at Amy's house on Walnut, she and Rachel told Amy goodnight. Then the two of them walked another quiet block together, and they too parted, and Samantha Longstreth was alone.

She hummed a tune she pieced together from an old movie. The song happened to be one famous in the mid-fifties, though she knew nothing beyond the melody—nothing of the starlet who sang it nor of the musical sharing the song's title. She absent-mindedly hummed and walked the four more blocks along Clay Street to Vine in the bitter cold, and then up the steep hill home.

Later, when she lay in bed with the lights out, she thought for the first time of the drowned boy, Stevie Lowe. It was strange that such an anonymous kid's death could make a gymnasium hush over, could cause strangers to mourn. If Stevie Lowe had lived a full life—if he'd grown to be one of those feed-capped, bib-overalled soybean farmers from Tripoli—his death would scarcely have registered in the town and county. People would have read about it in the paper and perhaps they would have said it was a shame. But certainly no one would have sobbed publicly the way some had in the gym after Mr. Tuttle made the announcement over the public address.

Because of the alphabetical proximity of their last names, Stevie had sat beside Samantha in countless classes and study halls over the years. But when she tried to remember him that night, she couldn't conjure his face or voice or laugh or anything about him. It was as if he'd not existed to her at all. Though of course sixteen hours before, he'd probably been sitting next to her in homeroom, though in recalling even that, her mind met with lethargy, entered a dimly lit space.

She gave up on all of it and finally closed her eyes and tried for a long time to sleep, but instead rolled around languidly for what might have been hours. When sleep finally did come, it was unrestful, and she sweated through her pajamas and sheets, and woke many times, hot and thirsty.

The day after Stevie Lowe died, Samantha rose late, still tired. Since her brother was in his first year of college, it was only Samantha and her parents left in the house. Her parents both worked early; her father was head miller at Kohl, Inc. and her mother a secretary at the county courthouse. They trusted Samantha to get up and go to school on her own. This had never been a problem; Samantha had had perfect attendance since ninth grade.

Today, however, she'd slept through what would've been second period and after she finally woke, she moved from room to room slowly, almost cautiously, as if she didn't know what might be lurking around the corner—a stranger, perhaps, drinking coffee, or someone sick on the floor, or a card game of elderly men. Any of it seemed possible.

Her mind was not the same today; something had happened. She ate some eggs and fell asleep again on the couch, watching a morning talk show, the last before the daytime soaps started, and she slept through the middle part of the day. Around two, she got up and showered and spread some homework on the dining room table, trigonometry, which she did quickly and easily. Samantha was a good student; math was her best subject.

She was sitting at the table reading about bicameral government when her parents arrived home separately within five minutes of each other. The evening rituals began then and she helped her mother prepare dinner while her father brought wood inside for the living-room stove. They ate quietly, all of them paying scant attention to the news on the television above the fridge; Samantha realized she felt no guilt for ruining her attendance record.

The next morning she was up before anyone, watching a national news show in the basement, the volume almost off. She sat bleary-eyed, hardly able to concentrate on the series of images floating past, now a heavily-clad correspondent in front of a nighttime Kremlin, now a flood-stricken town in Alabama where people stood on rooftops. "Nine dead in NE Alabama," a caption at the bottom of the screen read.

When she heard voices and footsteps stirring upstairs, she quietly left her cereal bowl on the floor and bundled up in an old scarf and an orange hunting coat she found in a downstairs closet. She grabbed her book bag and quietly left the house through the rear sliding-glass door just as her mother had begun to call down after all.

She descended into the wooded gully beyond the house in the dawn light, her breath billowing. Winter-hardened leaves cracked under her feet, and the noise of two distant dogs barking echoed through the empty trees.

The Highland River slowly snaked through the region and skirted the town in an ox-bow curve, nearly circumscribing it. Its headwaters were in the center of the state, and from there it ran to the southeast into the foothills, seemingly heedless of the rising terrain. Samantha had learned all about the river in an eighth-grade geology class, how it had once run in the opposite direction, emptying into the long-ago dead Teays, and then another dead river, the Mahomet, and finally into some prehistoric sea to the south.

But then the ice ages came and dammed the ancient river, sending the water spilling back into the hills, where new rivers were formed. The reversed water sometimes abandoned entire valleys as it steadfastly adhered to the principle of downhill flow. The idea that a river might change direction had captivated Samantha at a time when almost nothing sparked any real interest in her.

Though it was more than a mile out of her way to school, she found the spot where the boy had drowned. She had swum here herself in the summer, a deep place in the river with rocks to jump off and where huge channel catfish clung to the bottom in the summer heat. In the spare winter, though, the spot was transformed, practically unrecognizable. A path came right up to the water's edge, and you could see it continue on the other side of the river on into Reese Park, suggesting that one might just stroll across the water and pick up the path on the other side, as if the river were a minor obstruction.

Near the path, there was a scrap of particle-board attached to a large sycamore with shiny new nails. "Danger: Thin Ice," it read in sloppy orange spray-painted letters.

She pulled off a mitten with her teeth, leaned down, and touched the newly frozen ice near the shore. It cracked easily, its whiteness turning dark from the water beneath. When she touched the water, it was cold enough to be ice itself; the difference between ice and not-ice seemed almost arbitrary, though she knew it was a matter of scientific fact, more or less. She wiped her hand on her jeans and put the mitten back on.

Out in the water, she noticed a clear patch of jaggedness where Stevie had likely thrashed around before the coldness or fear or just plain disbelief had taken hold and sucked the energy from him. Standing, she tried to picture how he had come to the spot and looked across to the park, probably thinking he could just go on over. She imagined the look on his face—a relief, she realized, that she could remember anything about him—when his foot first gave way and he groped for something solid. He no doubt reached outward toward the fragile ice and deeper water instead of back, toward the cold dirt of shore.

She looked up and down the river, where the light through the beech trees cast broad, soft shadows on the ice. In the distance, she saw buses crossing the bridge on State 93. Time had gotten away from her.

She picked up a football-sized rock with both hands, swung its weight back and forth twice and then slung it as far as she could out onto the ice. It hit, bounced once, rolled some, and then sat motionless, suspended there.

"Stevie Lowe," she said. "Stevie Lowe."

She picked up her bag and climbed the bank and cut across a field in the direction of town and, ultimately, toward the high school. The sun rested above the hills now and shone down on Samantha as she joined the students migrating up Mulberry, the first street built in the town of her birth and life so far.

That morning, the day Stevie Lowe was to be buried, students quietly moped about in homeroom. At the request of the family only a small number of kids from the school—mainly family friends—were given passes to attend the event, but the mood was solemn and mournful anyway. Most sat in their seats without being told and listened to the morning announcements. A girl toward the back of the sprawling room sobbed quietly. The basketball team would travel to Hanover tomorrow, Mr. Holt said over the P.A.; the wrestlers had a home tournament over the weekend. The lunch today would be baked chicken with carrots and mashed potatoes. Have a good day.

Briefly Samantha looked down at the seat next to her where Stevie Lowe had sat. The kid on the other side of Stevie's seat, a boy named Chad, glanced at her. He was surreptitiously spitting tobacco juice into a Coke can; his lower lip bulged slightly. "Fuckin' A," he said. "Huh?"

She looked at him expressionless, no clue as to how to respond. He continued to nod anyway, as if she had agreed with him.

When the first bell rang, Samantha followed the winding stream of bodies out of the cavernous hall, down the bottlenecked aisle that led to the school's main building. Where the hallway emptied into a large locker area, she could hear someone wailing above the quiet, loud enough to be heard up and down the entire length of the hallway. Casting around, she saw Amy Schultz being tended to by two girls.

Samantha passed them with her eyes to the floor. At the end of the wide corridor, she ducked into the first-floor bathroom. Inside, some girls stood looking at themselves in the mirror, quietly talking about a television show in which a boy had died. Samantha stepped into one of the stalls and locked the door and waited until the late bell rang, then waited another few minutes before re-entering the empty hall and following a small corridor to the back of the school, to the stadium, and, beyond that, the streets of Moraine. If any teachers saw her, they did not bother to question her; she was a good student, a class officer, first-chair clarinet in the jazz band and orchestra. No one worried about Samantha Longstreth.

She wandered first toward the center of town, not any too sure of where exactly she intended to go. She went to Hebbing's Shoes and looked at a few pairs of flats but didn't stay long. Outside again, she took alleys and avoided the main avenue through town. She went to an out-of-the-way clothing shop near the light-bulb factory and spent most of her lunch money for the week on a shirt she'd seen a month before. She folded it up, stuck it in her backpack and walked on down Second to Williams Street and entered A&P at the side door. Nate Holland greeted her almost immediately; he stood close to the door stacking a display of peas. A year older than Samantha, Nate had already graduated.

"Hi," Samantha said.

"Samantha Longstreth," he said. "Skipping school?"

"Doctor's appointment," she explained. "I'm just killing some time."

He nodded his head firmly in understanding. He held two cans of peas in each hand.

She felt that Nate wanted to continue to talk, though he didn't appear to know how to prolong the conversation and they stood awkwardly for a long moment. "I suppose I should get back to this," he said, indicating with a nod toward the elevated manager's cubicle nearby.

"Right," she said and began to walk on. When she was a few steps away, he said her name and she looked back.

"That's crazy about Stevie Lowe, isn't it?" he asked.

He was wearing corduroys and a western shirt underneath a white, starched apron; everything about this store down to Nate himself seemed to have been plucked out of history, thought Samantha—the fifties, she guessed, or perhaps even before that.

She had the impulse to say something hateful to Nate about the dead boy. She didn't really know Stevie Lowe, she wanted to say. As close as she had sat to him all those years, she didn't know him, so why should she care any more about him than those people who drowned down South. But she didn't say any of those things. She told him she'd heard at the game.

"Man," he said, wearing a peculiar expression.

"It's weird," she said, then turned and walked on into the store, past the three checkout counters.

She was not really hungry but she picked out a three-pack of Slim Jims and a soft drink anyway. Then she remembered the shirt she'd bought and she set the items down on the breakfast cereal shelf and dug around in her pocket to see how much she had left. A dollar and thirty-one cents. She read the prices on the items: seventy-nine for the drink a dollar for the Slim Jims. What had seemed a whimsical treat a minute ago now seemed an absolute necessity. She quietly unzipped her backpack and placed both items inside. It would have to be all or nothing, she decided. She would never be able to pay for one while stealing the other.

She zipped the bag back up and started walking toward the front of the store. She walked around the end of the checkout counters and was heading for the door when a man's voice came from behind her.

"Miss, can I have a look inside your bag there?"

She passed Nate Holland then, his back to her, bent over his task.

She didn't even turn to the voice to see what the man looked like, to see if she knew him, too.

She broke into a sprint for the exit and the man yelled behind her: "Stop!" And then, a louder: "Stop her, Nathan!" She was on the sidewalk outside when she heard the man's voice one final time asking for someone to catch her.

She ran with no idea of what she was doing or where she was going. She followed the alley that ran behind the A&P and turned onto another perpendicular to it. Risking a look back, she saw no one behind her. She crossed a few streets, keeping to the alleyways. Some seven or eight blocks away, she stopped to rest in-between a garage and a tool shed that sat about three feet apart. The ground there was filled with large chunks of ceramic pipe from Moraine Clay Products. She leaned back against the shed and sat down and ripped open one of the Slim Jims. She pulled out the drink and washed the stringy meat down with it, quickly finishing the bottle.

For a long time, she sat there with eyes closed and listened, at first to her own breath and then to things outside herself—church bells chiming from a distant corner of town (it was half past some hour or another), the hum of trucks and cars along the distant highway. Nearby, she heard the suction of a basement door open and then someone hanging out clothes and the click of every clothespin as it fastened down on a shirt or pair of underwear.

After a while, she got up and began walking. The smell of coal was thick in the air of the neighborhood and she noticed its smoke issuing from most of the houses along Second and Garrison Streets. It was oppressive, that smell; it was the smell of winter and she longed for something, anything to take its place.

A faint sun had cut the chill of the morning some; she took off her coat and wrapped it around her waist. Already today she'd walked more than she had in months. She had no plan beyond walking, and she unconsciously arced toward home, passing through parts of Moraine she'd never really been in, not on foot, and she noted that they were not appreciably different than the parts she had.

2.

He stood on Williams Street with nothing to keep him warm but a long-sleeve shirt and an apron. Now that he'd stopped running, he felt the cold in his fingers. He was in front of Colson's Sunoco.

Why Samantha Longstreth would steal something from A&P didn't concern Nate in the least. Truth was, being away from work, even for only a short time, made him a little giddy. He felt grateful for the stunt. That it was cold and he was ill-suited for the coldness somehow deepened his giddiness. It was like stealing something himself.

He walked toward the river and made a large loop through town. As he walked he tried to recall what he had dreamed the previous night. He had only the feeling of it inside but could not come up with details. All he knew was that he'd woken with a light heart and in a better mood than usual. He took his time walking, even stopping at a gas station to buy gum.

Back on Williams Street, which ran in a nearly straight two-mile line from one end of town to the other, he took a long look to the east and was surprised to see Samantha Longstreth at some distance crossing Williams on either Carlisle or Corn Street, her orange hunting coat tied around her waist and unmistakable even at that distance.

He had known her for five or six years—casually, the way he knew hundreds of other kids at school. In all that time, he realized, he'd not given her a thought. Now, as she disappeared behind the theater and the sundry shop, he imagined a different, a whole person, replacing the superficial picture he'd kept of her, the yearbook facts; he gave her a history of his own imagining, placed her on vacation with her family on a trip to Tennessee. With a pleasant sort of jealousy, he imagined her kissing a boy working at an arcade's change desk. He imagined her singing in a church choir. "Hark the Herald Angels Sing!" He imagined her watching *The Shining*, expressions of fear filling her face.

He thought to run after her, but didn't. Instead he started to make his way back to the store. He'd been gone too long, he knew, and he wasn't sure if Mr. McCall would believe he had tracked the girl for so long, but over the past few months he had grown to care less about what Mr. McCall believed or wanted.

He was freezing now and the blocks back to the store seemed to stretch out forever. At the Y where Hunter Street splintered off from Williams, he ducked into an empty phone booth to get out of the wind for a minute. In Nate's lifetime, there had been all manner of Laundromats and bric-a-brac stores in the triangular building on the Y. Presently it was vacant and through the darkened windows he could make out cardboard boxes strewn about and a couple of armless mannequins.

He absently picked up the phone while he stood there and he read the witless graffiti scribbled on the booth wall in ballpoint and magic marker. *78 Kicks Ass. Shelia loves Mike. MegaDeth Rocks.*

"For a long distance call, dial 0 for the operator," read the text below the phone. He dialed "0." It was as easy as that. Soon a man's voice was on the line; Nate told him that he wanted to make a collect call.

"The number?"

Nate gave the man his brother's number, which he was surprised to remember, having called it only three or four times. Soon he heard the familiar voice talking to the operator about the charges. "Go ahead, sir," the operator said to Nate finally.

"Donnie," Nate said.

"Nate?" Donnie said groggily. "What's the matter?"

Nate saw that this had been a bad idea. Directly on the heels of that recognition, he remembered the three hour time difference.

"It's early there, idn't it?"

"It's okay," Donnie said. "We're up. We're getting up, anyway. We don't sleep all day."

"Nothing's wrong. I don't know. I just thought I'd call."

He looked out at the traffic moving along Williams. Cloud-cover hung over the valley obstinately.

"It's cold here," Nate said at last.

"Imagine it is, Junior. It's January. That's why they call it winter."

"What's it like out there?"

"You call about the weather, did you?"

"No," Nate said. He thought for a moment. "Stevie Lowe died in the river the other day."

"Who?"

"Aw, he was Kate Lowe's little brother, wadn't he? Stevie Lowe?" Nate only now made the connection between the dead boy and the girl his brother had dated for a summer some years back.

"Shit," Donnie said. "Stevie died?"

"He fell into the river down by the park," Nate said. "Through the ice."

"Shit," Donnie said again. "He couldn'a been more'n fourteen."

"He was a senior," Nate said.

"Nah."

"He was a year behind me."

"Goddammit, Nate. That's the worse news I heard in months." Nate could hear a woman's voice in the background and then Donnie said to her that he was talking to his kid brother. Nate had not met the woman; they had eloped after Donnie had finished basic training.

"I guess I thought you'd want to know," Nate said.

"Yeah, but it would be nice to hear from back there with good news on occasion."

"Well, sorry, Donnie. Bad news is the only kind we got today."

"Yeah. Alright. Bad news it is I guess."

"I should get off here, Donnie," Nate said. "I don't know what got into me. Money doesn't grow on trees."

"It's alright. I don't mind you calling." Then he asked, "You still working at the A&P?"

"No. I quit. Been looking around for something else. I was thinking of some classes at MCC."

"Now you're cookin' with gas," Donnie said. "You get your butt in gear on that." Donnie said something to his wife, but he must have been holding his hand over the receiver.

"I gotta go, Donnie," Nate said then.

"Hold on," Donnie said.

"Yeah?"

"Mom alright?"

"Yeah, she's fine," Nate said.

"Alright. Don't be a stranger."

Nate didn't bother going back inside A&P. Once he'd told his brother that he'd quit, he knew that that was what he wanted to do. He got into his Renault Alliance, a glorified golf cart; it had been a hand-me-down from Donnie.

He pulled onto Williams and then onto Fairfield and drove up the hill, passing the school with its squat stadium and baseball diamond. Some pitiful gym classes were standing out in the cold, shooting arrows at targets leaned against the steep bank bordering Hanock Avenue. He passed the old mayor's house, a place high on a hill made of the familiar ceramic brick produced locally at Moraine Clay since 1888. This date stuck firmly in Nate's head and probably everyone else's because it was emblazoned on billboards and softball T-shirts and restaurant placemats. You couldn't really forget when MCP had come into existence.

After Nate's father had retired from the tire plant he spent whole mornings at the Allegheny Inn, a diner near the fairgrounds connected to an old butcher shop. Nate had always felt comfortable there, and lacking any place to go now, he made his way through the residential area east of the school and city pool and tennis courts, down to Arlington Avenue and the Allegheny.

The restaurant's décor was nautical, despite the four hour drive necessary to get to any water you could launch a sea-going vessel in, and Nate saw when he stepped inside that the lighting was still dim, almost too dark to see. Decrepit wooden crate traps housing fake lobsters hung from the ceiling and on the walls oil-painted schooners banked under ominous skies. Three large aquariums sat near the entrance, filled mainly with goldfish.

Nate sat at his father's booth. Once upon a time, people actually avoided sitting there in the event that Arthur Holland would be stopping in, but the waitresses at the Allegheny had changed probably more than once since then and no one even recognized Nate as the son of Arthur Holland, which made Nate feel like much more than a year had passed since his dad had died.

Around eleven o'clock, the breakfast crowd thinned out, and soon there were no other customers besides Nate. The waitress occasionally came from behind a hidden coffee station to check on him. She refilled his coffee, took away dirty plates. She didn't seem bothered by his loitering as he sat reading through the Moraine and Atlas papers of the previous day.

Generally, Nate did not read the paper, but today it was enjoyable to stop and look outside of himself for a few hours; he spent the long shifts at the grocery deep in his own mind, perpetually running over the same thoughts. The release was liberating.

After scanning the papers from front to back several times, Nate turned now to the news of Stevie's death. It was in headlines at the top of page one in both papers. "Boy Drowns in Moraine," read one. "Moraine Youth Succumbs to Icy Water," read the other. The accounts were nearly identical.

Reading over the details, he saw that the Lowes still lived on

Backbridge Road, where he'd gone once with Donnie to pick up Kate—over two years ago now. The address caused something to click for Nate; until then, he hadn't considered a connection between Samantha Longstreth's behavior at A&P and the death of Stevie Lowe. But they were related, he knew almost instinctively.

He ran through all of it in his mind for a while. Finally, he paid for his breakfast and went to his car. He filled it with gas at a station across the street and then drove southeast along the river and eventually due south toward the Lowe's.

3.

Samantha found the keys to her brother's car in his room and then dug up some money she kept in a fat paperback—fifty-four dollars in fives and ones—and she left a short note on the counter to assuage any fears that she had slipped off the edge of the earth. Note or no note, her parents would worry; it couldn't be helped.

Outside, the wretched baby blue Rabbit choked to life. It needed a new exhaust system and transmission, she knew, which were at least two reasons why her brother wasn't allowed to have it at college. It coughed loudly as she gassed it. She didn't wait for it to warm and pulled onto Vine Street, throwing gravel into the yard.

Running a typically long red light at Clemson Avenue, she drove past the factories along the river and crossed to the other side of the valley. She passed the golf course and a series of summer Scouting camps and then drove on into the hills on a small road she knew.

At a new convenience store south of town, Samantha used the bathroom and then found the payphone next to the rear exit. An open utility room stacked floor to ceiling with boxed cleaning supplies stood across the small aisle. She looked up all of the Lowes in Moraine County in the thin white pages. There were four, two with city addresses. Those were out; Stevie, she knew—whether from his boots or clothes or his absence on snowy days, she couldn't say—was from the country.

Of the remaining two Lowes, one was named Harlan, on Backbridge Road, the other Carl, on Swine Road. Samantha considered calling them to find out which was Stevie's family. She looked around the store. The boy behind the register was watching TV and stealing glances back at her. You didn't call up someone to ask them if their son was dead, she thought.

She wrote down the two addresses on her hand with a dirty Bic pen she found lying on a nearby shelf. She'd never heard of either road, and she couldn't imagine where she might get a county map. On the way out the door, she stopped and asked the boy at the counter if he knew the addresses. He didn't.

Out in the countryside, she passed a steady stream of roads whose names seemed pulled from some mythical Scottish landscape—Cartwright, Dickson, Lombard, Brodie. Eventually, she came into tracts of Amish farms, people who'd moved into the area in the last decade or two, buying up land here and there, paying, Samantha had heard, with cash. In the fall, these Amish bailed hay like in the old times, creating the pyramidal bundles that stood in the fields drying as in some painting from Europe. The Amish fascinated her father; he would drive the family by the farms sometimes, and speak admiringly of the resolve of these people, their commitment to a way of life.

Samantha wove her way out of the Highland Valley and through the hills, searching out the family of the dead boy. It was a ridiculous pursuit. Had she stopped to weigh things, she might have found all manner of reasons for turning around. The sensible world of two days ago had evaporated like softly spoken words, though, and she moved on unquestioningly. And maybe this was it: she had believed—and had been led to believe—that people were all alike somehow, that in some fundamental way, they were all the same. Out there in the hills, she moved through the mid-morning dreariness without any real sense that she belonged here or had commonalities with any living thing and, perhaps, she needed to understand this better.

She banked now on guidance from some knowledge inside that she hadn't been aware of before.

4.

At the house, Nate parked on the road and watched the activity there for a while. He looked for any sign of Samantha and he waited. He watched for some time before it at last occurred to him that the funeral was taking place here; trucks and cars first filled the long driveway, and then parked haphazardly in the frozen grass.

Though it seemed to Nate disrespectful to enter the house when all he wanted was to find a girl, he soon pulled his car into the accruing mess of automobiles and walked the long lane to the house.

He followed an older couple around to a low, sprawling porch that led to a rickety screen door. He walked in right behind the aging couple, as if he were their grandson, come along to mourn the boy.

The couple stopped and took off their coats and hung them on hooks in a large anteroom filled with everything from lawn furniture to an old-style washing machine, replete with hand-operated wringing pins. Nate left his coat on. He found a spot in a corner near a refrigerator and stood gazing around the place, noting that more people seemed to be arriving all the time.

A man from Huntington, some distance to the south, began speaking to Nate. For reasons Nate failed to apprehend, the man was talking about atomic energy, about the difference between forging and storing it. As if prompted by a student's questions, he explained to Nate about weapons-grade plutonium, its dangers.

A large, bearded man moved about the kitchen, cradling a half-dozen beers in his untucked shirt, dispensing them without discrimination. He made eye contact with Nate and then extended a bottle toward him. Nate took it and looked back to the atomic man, who said, "In my book, if you're old enough to die in some godforsaken jungle, then you're old enough for one of those." Seamlessly, the atomic talk resumed; the man eventually revealed that he had recently retired after forty years in an atomic energy plant. When he looked to Nate for a response Nate's mind clouded over.

"My brother's in the Army," he said at last. "Out to the Mojave."

The man nodded knowingly, like he too might have spent a grueling season or two in the service of Uncle Sam in some similarly barren landscape.

"It's a hell of a place," the man said. "Hot."

Nate confirmed this with a nod. He knew almost nothing about the place except this very fact.

As quickly as he had appeared before Nate, the man disappeared, and now Nate was on a second beer, handed to him by the same roving benefactor. Across the room, a phone was ringing loudly—an old black box of a thing that might have once been the kind used in factories, such was the volume of its ring. Nate saw a woman answer it as she looked out the kitchen window onto the joyless overcast day. Then Nate saw Kate Lowe approaching him.

"You're Nate," she proclaimed when she stood in front of him. She wore a navy dress and a pearl necklace with matching earrings; she was beautiful, Nate thought. Even if he had not known her, his eyes would have fallen on her.

"Yeah," he told her. "I'm Nate. And you're Kate."

The mere three years between them had felt like ten to Nate during the times she had come around the house with his brother. He had been intimidated to the point of silence, in fact—something very powerful, some unspeakable confidence in her. Now he discovered that despite having graduated from high school himself, the feeling had not dissipated.

"Donnie's brother," Kate said, confirming.

"That's right," he said.

"I didn't realize you were close to Stevie," she said. "I've not seen too many kids from the school here." Her hands were clasped in front of her at waist height, the way a practiced minister's hands might be. She looked around the room quickly as if to double-check her facts.

He meant to say something, but nothing came at first.

"I'm sorry about Stevie," he said finally.

"Come here," she told him. "I want to show you something."

She walked down a hall, past several closed doors, and led Nate into a blue room where spare light leaked in through closed curtains and only in the vaguest way revealed a made bed and an armchair and a number of various dressers and shelves. She closed the door and then walked over near Nate. He tensed, but did not move.

"I heard Donnie was out to California," she said.

"Barstow."

"What's he doing way out there?"

Nate tried to make out Kate in the partial light. It was tough going. He thought he could see her freckles, but most of her features he constructed from memory.

"He's in the army."

She rolled her eyes, a little flustered. "I know he's in the stupid army," she said. "Is he not going to move back to Moraine?" The story was beginning to clear up for Nate. Kate did not know that Donnie had gotten married.

"I don't know," he told her.

"He's going to wake up some day and see that he's missed everything. And for what?"

Nate shrugged, though he knew she probably couldn't see him. Nothing was too reliable here. The dark room was just one more factor adding to this lack of clarity. Something inside told him that Kate was on the verge of tears.

She stepped closer then and lifted her head to him and kissed him on the mouth. She did not touch him otherwise and he did not move away.

Her eyes were closed—the first thing he could see with any certainty—
and she seemed to find release in this kiss, gently running her tongue
along his. He had known nothing like it.

The kiss lasted a long moment. Afterward, Kate stepped away and
looked at him, again camouflaged by darkness, and moved toward the
door.

"Stevie's body is in the next room," she said. "If you want to pay
your respects."

She opened the door and daylight came in and he caught a glimpse
of her sliding past the entrance. The door closed and he was alone and
only then did it occur to him that he was standing in Stevie's bedroom.
He walked to the window and pulled open the curtain a little, revealing
on a shelf below it some framed group photos of Stevie: band camp,
youth baseball, 4H.

Nate had not known Stevie Lowe had been in 4H, though of course
he had—all country kids were in 4H and FFA. He also did not remember
playing baseball against Stevie, but looking at the photo a little closer, he
recognized Stevie's team—Rotary International—and recognized, too,
several of the other boys on the team—Chad Holt, Russ Dix, Sherman
Brookwater, boys Nate played baseball and basketball and football with
for years—and he was sure he had played against this very team one
summer night between fifth and sixth grade. He managed to excavate
them from memory now, pulling up first faces he remembered easily and
then some he was surprised to retrieve, and then actual events: a catch
he had made of a line drive; a pop fly he had lost in the lights. He had
drawn a walk at least once that night, and he remembered standing
behind the backstop as his GE teammate John McCaslin hit a ball
farther than he'd ever seen one hit.

He thought he remembered his own father yelling for him to keep
his head up after a strikeout, a called third strike—the worst of offenses—

and he had returned to the dugout with his head lowered like some cartoon failure, and then his father had yelled from the stands.

That night, in the late innings, when coaches cleared their benches because league rules mandated that everyone got to play at least two innings, Stevie Lowe appeared in the Rotary batting order and in right center field. Nate could see him now, remembered his tiny figure as he squatted, at his coach's urging, so that his strike zone was impossibly small, completely unattainable for the twelve year-old pitchers. Stevie walked once late in that game and had stood on first base as the next three batters had struck out and Nate's team, GE, had won.

Did he mean to come here and grieve with these people for the loss of their small, silent son?

Maybe he did not yet have that sort of grief in him. Perhaps it was lurking too far inside, buried since his father had died and his mother had slipped away into a silent spot next to the turned-off television, where she had begun reading about tulips.

Soon, Kate's final words hit Nate. Stevie was there, right next door.

5.

It was already afternoon when by nothing more than chance Samantha found the improbably named Swine Road; there must've been another eighty some roads in the county she hadn't driven on or by. She traveled the nine miles of its length until, at its end, she arrived at the address of Carl Lowe.

She pulled to the side of the road and watched the house. There were chickens in the yard, but nothing else moving. A wagon and truck sat in front of the place. There was nothing happening here. She sat for a long while, and then slowly drove on. Almost immediately, Swine dead-ended into Backbridge. She turned right and the first house was 3343 Backbridge, Harlan Lowe's address. The other Lowe house was still in view, a quarter of mile or so distant, the two families clearly somehow related.

Samantha pulled into a crowded driveway and parked behind a Grand Torino. There were hordes of cars there, and people in the yard as well. Samantha did not hesitate. She got out and moved through the yard and into the house without thought or self-consciousness. Inside, she entered a kitchen, wall to wall with people and heavy with the smell of burned coffee. Everyone stood around and talked, not so quietly as she might've imagined. Somewhere in a distant room there was banjo music. Samantha wandered from room to room, perfectly at ease among the strangers. She met a small group of boys she recognized from school, but they paid her no attention and she walked on and approached a young boy of perhaps eight.

"Do you know where the boy's mother is?" she asked him.

He looked at her. "What boy?"

"The drowned boy," she said. She couldn't say his name; it sounded wrong in her head, though "the drowned boy" did, too, now that she heard it.

"Stevie's mom?" the boy said.

"Yes."

"Stevie's my brother."

He seemed to register her shock.

"I'm sorry," she said. "I didn't know. I was just looking." Her voice trailed off.

"What's your name?" the boy asked.

"Samantha."

"Samantha," he repeated oddly, and then he turned and ran out of the crowded room. She looked around herself, somehow vulnerable now.

6.

Stevie's body was in a small room in the center of the house. There were no windows, only a bulbous skylight high overhead that had obviously been added in recent years and seemed to have been poorly installed from the looks of the dark water stains slanting down the pitched ceiling away from it, disappearing where they met the dirty sheet-rock walls.

The room was occupied by a handful of solemn women, one of whom Nate took to be Stevie's mother. She resided over a homemade casket lined with an intricately-designed quilt. Once in the room, Nate stood awkwardly as he tried to sort out what to do and how to act. Nobody seemed to pay any attention to him, though, so he approached the casket.

He stood close enough to Stevie's corpse to see the creases in the boy's lifeless face. Nate's only point of comparison for all of this was of course his father, who had been made up as he lay in the coffin, wearing the thick powdery dust that gave him a false color. It had made him nearly unrecognizable, in fact, his face somehow the wrong size and shape, his mouth unnaturally drawn. Stevie's mouth, too, was shut, but by a stack of pillows that tilted his chin against his chest. He wore no makeup, and despite the vacuity in his face, Nate could see the likeness to the boy he vaguely remembered, even to the much younger boy from the photographs.

Nate stood over the coffin for what he hoped was a long enough time. His mind wandered to his father again, whom he had willfully thought little about. As if merely seeing another dead body had opened up some gate, a wave of grief swept through Nate and he fought for a moment against tears.

He did not want to be here feeling these things in front of people who today had their own grief. He turned and crossed the stuffy room toward the door and ventured to look up at the women as he did so and met the eyes of one of them, perhaps an aunt or some more distant relative.

For her, as for Kate, Nate had nothing to give, nothing to say. The woman soon looked away, perhaps seeing in him that he was no more with her in that room than Stevie himself, and Nate left the way he'd come in, moving back toward the kitchen and the living room where most of the guests had congregated.

7.

Down the hall, Nate stood before Samantha Longstreth, struggling to regain his composure. They were both a little shocked to see the other, a fact that somehow diffused the situation.

"Samantha," he said. The very sound of her name carried meaning for him now.

The little boy was back and stood next to Samantha again. Nate immediately recognized him as a blood relation of Stevie Lowe— something in the cheeks and nose. The boy stood looking at Samantha at first, but then turned toward Nate.

Nate was taken aback by the frankness of his gaze.

"Do you know what will happen to Stevie now?" he said.

Nate shook his head.

Instead of answering his own question, as Nate expected him to, the boy exhaled a strange cackle and ran off into the crowd again. Nate and Samantha stood by themselves. Nate saw now, standing near her, that he merely wanted to see her; he had nothing to pledge or promise.

"Why are you here?" she asked.

He tried to find a smile—one that would seem appropriate. He just didn't know what to say to this girl; she might as well have been from another country.

"I came to find you," he said.

"You did not."

He nodded.

"You did not drive all the way out here for that."

"I did," he said, but then he realized she thought he was talking about the stolen items. "Not," he started, but a man emerged from the roiling living room then, as if spit out like a lottery ball, and took Nate by the arm gingerly. It was the uniformed Army recruiter who Donnie had talked to about joining the army.

"Mr. Holland," he said dramatically. "How's things?"

He did not seem too grieved. A full beer bottle dangled from the pinky of his left hand.

"I'm fine," Nate said. He didn't know how to address the man, whose name was Sergeant Hanson.

"What's the latest from your bro'?" he asked.

As the man spoke to Nate, Samantha stepped away—did not really even excuse herself, just stepped back and turned, and moved toward a door. Nate watched her go and thought to grab her or excuse himself but Hanson interrupted his thought, put his hand on Nate's shoulder.

"Never mind the skirt for a minute here, Holland," Sergeant Hanson was saying.

"I ain't heard from Donnie," Nate told him.

"Well, if he's in California, he's doing alright. You know what I'm saying?"

Nate smiled politely and looked around, wondering where Samantha could have gone.

"It's a fuckin' shame about Stevie, idn't it?" Hanson said.

"Yeah," said Nate.

"He was heading down to Benning come June," said Hanson. "He wanted to go Airborne."

"Yeah?"

"I think he had the makings of a real badass, between you and me."

Hanson drank from his beer.

"Stevie was pretty slight," Nate observed, not really wanting to argue about Stevie's physical prowess at his funeral, but annoyed somehow that Hanson wanted to.

"Yeah," Hanson said, "but it's the slight ones, you see. They're the ones who do the real ass-kicking."

Nate nodded. He would not take it any further.

"Like you," Hanson said. "I bet with a little training, a little strengthening, you could beat some serious ass."

"Why would I want to?" Nate asked.

"You never know when you need to beat some ass, Nathan. It's Nathan, right?"

"Nate."

"Nate then. You never know when you might need to open up a can of you know what."

"When was the last time you had to beat someone's ass?" Nate heard himself say.

"Last night," Hanson said and waited for Nate to respond. When he didn't, Hanson went on. "No," he said. "I don't find myself in much trouble anymore. I'm not as young as I used to be. But let's say I was over in Mogadishu. Bunch of Muslims fucking with me."

"Why would you be over there?" Nate said. He was starting to feel a strong need to leave the house.

"If I was in the Army, Nathan. If I was over there on a mission and something happened and I was by myself."

"But what if you didn't want to be in the Army. Why would you need to beat anyone's ass then?"

"I'm just making a point here. There are times and places when it is handy—when it is valuable—to be able to beat ass."

"I haven't been there," Nate said. He looked around the room. "Look, Sergeant Hanson. I've gotta run."

"She's not going anywhere," Hanson said.

Like hell, Nate thought. That's exactly what this girl does: she goes. She disappears.

"You come visit me down on First Street sometime," Hanson said. "I know it's not the path your brother wants to travel, but the U.S. government will pay for every last penny of your tuition if you want to go to college. I figure you to be the type to want an education?"

"I don't know," Nate told him.

"Stop down," Hanson said again. "That's what I'm there for. To help out young men like yourself."

"Okay," Nate said finally.

"Good," Hanson said. "You do that. You come down and we'll talk about the possibilities, the almost inconceivable things you could do in this world."

"Alright," Nate said. "Alright." And he slipped away through a door that led him to a mudroom and then he was on the porch, a little buzzed. Dark, dense clouds had moved in over the funeral and it had started to spit snow.

He found the way to his car down the long drive and saw a quagmire of automobiles; it looked like a junkyard, except that all of these vehicles presumably ran, or at least had in the preceding hours. He saw that while his car wasn't in the absolute worst position, there was no way he would be able to get it out. It was cold and he returned to the house.

8.

Through the next room and into a third, Samantha was looking for her way back to the entrance she'd come in ten minutes before.

A man in his thirties noticed her. "You need something, hon?" he asked.

He seemed too young to call her "hon," but there apparently hadn't been a good alternative to his mind.

"I was looking for the bathroom," she managed.

"That's what I thought," he said. "Second door down this here hallway." He pointed to a dark hall off the old run-down dining room they were in.

"Thank you," she said.

Inside the bathroom, she locked the door behind her and sat down on the closed toilet. A corrugated plastic window filtered opaque light. Samantha tried to collect her thoughts.

If she had come to see the dead boy, it had been a mistake; she saw that now.

When she slid the window open by five or six inches, she saw that there were five men standing in the yard nearby, drinking beer, their free hands stuffed into the pockets of their pants.

She closed it and steeled herself. Back in the crowd, she looked at the floor as she walked. She'd have to hit an exit eventually. Houses could not be infinite; another fact of science. She breathed deeply, from the diaphragm, as she'd learned to do in speech class, and she tried to avoid the room where she'd seen Nate. Soon she was on the dilapidated back porch.

There were men here, too—also drinking beer. Perhaps it was the same men, moved around from the other side of the house. There was no way of telling; everyone looked the same. It was cold. She walked through the yard toward her car, down the long driveway. The Rabbit was blocked in by a GMC truck. Samantha stood and looked at the configuration of cars for some time and finally saw where she might be able to nose through two cars and get out by way of the yard. She did this, angling up onto the road through a ditch and dragging her car's underside some in the process, but now she was on Backbridge, southbound. It was not at all relief she felt to be on the road again, as she'd hoped, but dread in some all-encompassing form. It seeped in and threatened to overcome her.

The terrain itself bore little resemblance to the earth she knew, but was some other world contrived in part by her very brain chemistry, in part by the clouding skies and geological events long since passed. She envisioned the landscape unwrapping in front of her as if she were sitting still and the land itself were the thing moving. This perception seemed in line with the rest of her state of mind and she accepted it stoically. She had no yardstick by which to measure things, and so she accepted it all and drove south and expected the worst. The one bit of clarity was that she needed to escape, to get away from everyone and everything she knew.

At Keller and Gallia, she stopped and the car idled roughly. The car's heater was finally throwing warmth over her legs. The fields that lined this valley seemed to stretch relentlessly in the cold. Each row of dirt and dead cornstalk harbored some residual snow from a Christmas storm and now, adding to that, fresh snow fell and Samantha sat at the crossroad and calmed down.

She put the car in gear and pulled on through the stop sign, fiddling with the radio until she found a pop station from a distant city to the north. A commercial advertised a condominium in Myrtle Beach where the owner of the radio station vacationed—for free, no doubt, in exchange for this very commercial—and before the commercial even ended, the road climbed out of the valley and into the hills, and the station faded, almost as if it had been purposefully cut off by some knowing hand. Then, slowly trolling the FM band with one hand and steering with the other, all she could find were a couple country stations. She turned it off.

At Maine Road, she randomly went left, and then right on Samuels and right again on McDaniels. She took another left at a Y onto Old Ashton Road. When she came into view of the green signs marking the municipality of Ashton, though, she pulled into a driveway and turned around and returned the way she'd come.

On Furnace Road, she stopped at an old gas station just past the intersection and put in five dollars of gas, which nearly filled the small tank.

The gas station was in an old farm house, decrepit and painted white in the spots where paint still clung to the wood. Inside, the station was dirty and the woman at the counter smoked, cloudy tendrils rising from a Merit 100s plastic ashtray sitting on the counter next to an old-fashioned cash register. On the walls, two deer heads and one jackalope hung. Paul Harvey spoke through a small transistor radio behind the counter, complaining about the arrogance of a Californian congressman.

"Afternoon, sweetheart," the woman behind the counter said. Time hadn't entered Samantha's mind all morning, and now it was apparently past twelve.

"Afternoon," Samantha said to the woman.

"Gonna snow some, ain't it?" the woman said. Samantha looked behind the woman toward the window and the day beyond, as if she'd forgotten the outside world entirely in the thirty seconds since she'd left it.

"Yeah," she said at last. "I believe so."

She walked to the drinks station and poured herself a coffee and put in a lot of sugar and half and half, and then walked back over to the counter.

"That and the gas is all?"

"And these," she said, picking up some powdered donuts from a rack in front of the counter. As the woman figured the sum on a pocket calculator—the old cash register apparently did not work—Samantha scanned the place for some article of interest to rest her eyes upon. She found only a large Mickey Mouse clock, broken, or at least unplugged.

"That's six-fifty," the woman said.

Samantha handed the woman ten dollars.

"You visitin' some family down this way?" the woman asked.

Samantha said nothing, only looked at the woman confused.

"Oh, I just seen that your plates was from up to Moraine County, hon. I'm not keepin' tabs on no one."

"Oh," Samantha said. "I'm just out for a drive."

"That's nice," the woman said. "Not the prettiest day for it, but better 'n some."

Samantha nodded. A single wooden chair sat beside the magazines, a knee-high ashtray next to it. Samantha sat in the chair and opened the donuts and began eating them one at a time. The woman stood over behind the counter smoking, snorting once or twice at Paul Harvey's witticisms.

"You out of school, then?" she asked Samantha after some time had passed.

"Yep."

"Couldn't hardly of been out for more than a year or two," she observed, as if awoken from a sleep.

"One year," Samantha said, enjoying the lie some.

"Gotta boyfriend, I bet."

"Nah," she said. "I'm taking it all slow. I'm just out seeing my country."

Years ago she had heard her father say this to a sheriff's deputy who had picked them up for speeding on some similar back roads. It had seemed to satisfy the deputy, who wondered what had brought them to that remote stretch of road, and seemed to Samantha, furthermore, an answer as good in one situation as many others.

"Well," the woman responded proudly. "Good for you, darlin'. I wish I'd done more a that."

When she had finished the entire roll of donuts, she stood and found a trash can and threw away both the empty coffee and donut wrapper.

"Thank you," she told the woman.

"It's good to have some company now and again," the woman told her.

"I imagine so," Samantha said and smiled. She started for the door, but then felt a terrible sickness rising inside. A stricken look must have crossed her face, because the woman put her cigarette down and came out from behind the counter.

"What's a matter, hon?" she said. "You all right?"

Samantha shook her head and made her way back to the chair, and it was all she could do to fall into it.

"What do you need, hon?"

Samantha couldn't speak at first.

A few minutes went by, but the feeling did not fade. She felt dizzy now, and nauseated. "There a bathroom?" she muttered.

"Sure," the woman said. She led Samantha down a hallway lit by a low watt bulb. She could hear loud rock music back here, its percussion allied with her illness, increasing her nausea as they seemed to approach the source.

Now her vision, too, began to fail, and she leaned on the woman almost entirely. "I can't see," she murmured, and was aware of the confusion in her voice; she felt like she couldn't breathe either. She struggled to keep alongside the woman, determined to make it to the bathroom, though it seemed they had been on the march to it for a long time.

She could still hear the woman and the music and their own footsteps on the hardwood, but now could not see at all and she closed her eyes a number of times, as if to clear them, and then finally left them shut as they were doing her no good anyway.

They turned down several hallways—the music's noise modulating, now louder, now softer—until they finally turned into a room, which she recognized as a room because carpet muted the music—shag carpet, she was almost sure.

"I'm right here, honey," the woman said, steering her across the room. She led her to the toilet, placing her hand on the top of the closed bowl.

Samantha lifted the lid and lowered herself to the floor, and then began to retch—the donut, the coffee, the Rice Crispies, the Slim Jims, all of it. She gagged until she thought she was done, and then she gagged two or three more times, her small body heaving, nothing left to produce. She was dizzy and drained, and still could not see. The woman was running water in the sink now, and she said, "Here," and Samantha lifted her hand in the direction of the voice, and was handed a wet washcloth. "I'm sorry," she told the woman.

"Hush," the woman said kindly. "Now we'll need to get you to a bed, get you rested up before you carry on with your grand tour."

Samantha wanted to object, but she could marshal no words. More than anything she really just longed for the bed of which the woman spoke, and it didn't matter how dirty it was or how many animals she'd have to share it with.

"Take my hand now," the woman said, and then she had Samantha by the arm again and guided her out of the room and ushered her into another. She pulled off Samantha's coat and scarf.

"You just lie down here," she said, and Samantha did as she was told, moving slowly. When she was supine, the woman pulled off her shoes and draped a blanket over top her. "I'll be back to check on you in a bit," the woman said, and then turned the light off. Before the woman had left the room, Samantha had lost consciousness entirely.

9.

Atomic Energy Man met Nate at the backdoor, not far from where they'd had their first conversation; it was as if they gravitated toward one another. Cigarette smoke drifted from room to room as if on wind.

"In Rome," the man was saying, "if you were poor and knew you wouldn't be able to afford a funeral, you joined a funeral club. Collegia Funeraticia, they called it. Kind of a toastmasters setup. You went to these monthly meetings and paid dues, et cetera. And then when you died, you got your funeral paid for and the folks in your funeral club came as the mourners."

Nate watched the man speak. Escalating voices rode a banjo from the next room. On a wall near them, there was a framed painting of three ships, perhaps the Niña, the Pinta, and the Santa Maria.

"Ain't that something?" the man said. "A fricken' funeral club?"

Nate nodded, and then asked the man, "You related to Stevie?"

"Wife is. She was his great aunt, I believe. Previous marriage."

"You ever meet him?"

"I don't think so," he started, but then corrected himself. "Well. Maybe. At one of these big picnic affairs down to Malta on the river."

"He played baseball," Nate said.

"Oh yeah? We didn't spend a lot of time with this side of the family."

Outside the nearest window, Nate could see the Lowe family forming a circle in front of an above-ground pool. A light, steady snow fell. He noted Kate out there, as well as an older brother, two other sisters, and the little boy who'd been with Samantha—Stevie's youngest brother, no doubt. Stevie's parents were there, too, dressed in solemn black clothes that looked to have been made in a time long since passed.

The father, Nate remembered now, was a minister, and he had them all holding hands and was speaking with his head bowed. Beyond them myriad outbuildings of every size and shape littered the property, and scattered about in every direction were rusting farm implements and a number of abandoned lawn mowers and smaller parts that Nate took in his ignorance of things mechanical to be carburetors and alternators and engine blocks. Beyond all of this agricultural and mechanical flotsam, stark hills rose all at once out of the valley, miniature mountains, the trees of which were unthinkably dark against some stubborn snow patches. And there he saw, on a small area of the hillside, the family cemetery, not more than twenty-five tombstones clustered together near the tree line. At the corner of the cemetery a yellow backhoe rested beside a mound of freshly dug earth.

"Life's as cheap as sticks," Atomic Energy Man told Nate now, taking note of the family congregating in the backyard. "With all respect to the deceased. A single life isn't worth much. Yours. Mine."

Nate looked at the man. "What?"

"Sweep of history, see. The whole collection of things. Culture. Art. Music. We're nothing by ourselves."

Nate pondered this for a moment, but then the man interrupted his thought. "Is it hot in here?" he asked.

Nate nodded. It was unbearably hot.

Nate excused himself and he roamed about the house, past the room that held Stevie's body, past the kitchen, a sewing room, other bedrooms, the banjo players. At first, maybe he was looking for an exit, but that idea passed, and he just moved, like an apparition, swimming from room to room in an endless series of loops.

Stevie Lowe. Like Nate's own father, he would soon disappear into the earth forever, never to be heard from again—an incomprehensible idea. Only in thoughts—only in the minds of those living—would Stevie exist. A pain had opened up inside Nate and the movement dulled it. So he moved.

As he lapped through the house, he grew familiar with certain faces;

he noted the music's rising volume, the transformation of the slack-jawed people, their complexions turning red, their eyes opening toward one another in wide, focused expressions. He didn't notice, as he continued to move, that he had begun to draw attention to himself, his odd bird-like circling. A woman watched him cross the floor in the old dining room for the thirtieth or fortieth time and she stared at this conspicuous gray sweat-shirted boy. Had Samantha appeared in front of Nate, he probably wouldn't have stopped. He was not interested in Samantha, he saw now. It was something else entirely.

Soon a thin man had Nate by the arm and asked him if he needed to step outside. Nate said that he did, and the two of them exited the house together, where the snow fell in huge flakes. Nate stepped away from the man, who seemed to guard the door, preventing him from going back inside. There was a group of men and children sitting in lawn chairs out in the cold and snow where he had earlier witnessed the Lowes in their prayer circle. The men were smoking, talking quietly, respectfully, but it felt to Nate like the whole of the house was a tinderbox, everyone ready to lose some sane part of themselves.

Nate stood and watched the storm come in, grateful to have a chance to escape the funeral.

As he warmed the engine, a family parked beside him and got out of their van. The kids—a boy and a girl—wore Oakland Raiders coats, which were soiled thoroughly, presumably from playing touch football or sliding down gulley banks. The mother looked at Nate, a sort of half smile.

"What a time for a snowstorm," she said.

Nate looked at her with a dazed expression. It was a perfect time for a snowstorm, he thought. There had been no more perfect time in his nearly twenty years.

He ransacked the glove box of his car and found a map of the county—he had inherited many curious maps and other oddities from his brother in the glove box, but this was the first time he'd ever found use for any of them. He spread the map out on his hood and studied it the way a surveyor might, the paper vibrating from the engine's idle. He found his location easily and he surveyed the region nearby, as if he were searching for points of interest. He might just end up anywhere. He would aim south, he decided. The direction mattered less than the movement.

10.

When Samantha woke, two unfamiliar women were standing over her with a tray of food. It required several moments for her to piece together how she had ended up here, remembering the morning's tangled logic and the clerk at the gas station at the end of it. The rest came to her more slowly—the sickness, the blindness, the bathroom, the bed. She could see again, she only then realized.

"You diabetic?" the woman with the clerk asked. She looked elderly, or on the verge of it.

Samantha shook her head. The woman busied herself with the tray on the stand next to Samantha's bed. "Go get her a paper towel, Doreen," she said, and Doreen disappeared and returned a moment later with a white roll of paper towels, and tore off two and set them next to Samantha.

"This is some chicken soup and fried baloney," said the older woman.

"What time is it?" Samantha asked.

"You need to be somewheres?" the older woman asked.

"No," Samantha said.

"Your folks live up to Moraine County, do they?"

"They're dead," Samantha said.

"Ah hon," Doreen said. Then to the older woman: "You quit badgerin' her. She just needs to eat some and could do without the third degree."

Samantha felt like she was going to fall asleep again while the women were there arguing about her. She picked at the sandwich, eating bits of the bread, then tasting and spitting out the meat. She ate a few spoonfuls of the soup.

Doreen was now standing at the door, trying to usher the other woman out of the room. "You holler if you need something," she said. "We're just down the hall." Samantha nodded meekly. The older woman looked back at her with suspicion or maybe scorn, but then the two of them disappeared, leaving the light on so she could see to eat.

Samantha slumped back into the bed then and slipped into a dream of the fevered.

When she woke again, she did so with a whispered moan. After some minutes, she sat up and pulled the curtains back to find a bricked-in window. It could have been two o'clock or nine; she didn't have the first indication either way.

She heard voices coming from down the hall, including a man's.

She felt sick again. She got out of bed and, shivering without the blankets, she found her way to the bathroom and again voided her stomach. Afterward she washed out her mouth and washed her hands and would have examined her face, but there was no mirror.

Out in the hall, she heard a door slam and she walked toward the voices; she even then listed from some imbalance. She came upon the room where the same two women stood looking out the window. Hearing her, they immediately turned. Samantha could see snow coming down outside in a cartoonish density. A man sat in a high-back chair on the other side of the room, smoking and reading a newspaper.

"You look like death warmed over," the older woman said.

"That's our traveler, huh?" the man said.

Doreen came toward Samantha. "How you feel, hon?"

Samantha could only nod that she was okay. She focused on the snow outside and saw, upon closer study, several figures moving away from the house.

The older woman, whom Samantha assumed was Doreen's mother or mother-in-law, looked out the window again. "Them people ought to know better," she said.

"What's the matter?" Samantha asked. She leaned her back against a red arched doorway. Doreen stood very close to her, as if she might catch her were she to fall.

"You need to lie back down," Doreen said.

"Been an accident," the older woman said, turning around. "We should call your relatives cause you're not going to be driving in this."

"You from up to Moraine or Falls or where?"

"Moraine," she said.

"How come you're driving around down here in a snowstorm?"

She shrugged. "Wasn't a snowstorm when I left."

"Did you know a . . ." He stopped and looked at the headlines of the paper. "A Stevie Lowe?"

"No," Samantha said.

"Well he died in the river. Up to Moraine."

She and the man watched each other as a boy came in through the front door and said that the guy driving the cart—the Amish man—was dead, or nearly so. He wasn't moving anyway. He didn't look to be living, the boy said.

"Good lord," the older woman said.

Doreen was already on the phone, which hung from a wall near the door. She was explaining to a dispatcher that there'd been a wreck involving a small Toyota truck and an Amish buggy on Furnace Road.

"You need to get back to bed," Doreen told her when she got off the phone. She had her by the arm again.

She led Samantha back to the room, but when Doreen disappeared again to go deal with the accident, Samantha put on her boots and collected her clothes and began moving down the corridor in the direction she imagined the store to be in. It took some doing, but eventually she found it. She passed a man at the main counter.

"Hello, there," the man said, like he wanted to say more and was just waiting for the go-ahead.

"Hi," she responded blankly, and then pulled on her hat and gloves and without looking back at the man, she opened the door, which jingled a belt of Christmas bells, and then she stepped outside and let the door slam behind her.

Outside it was dark, a dreamscape of snow—a different place entirely. Not only was the gas station from earlier that day buried now beyond recognition, but it seemed as if she'd stumbled into a different country. Gone were the ubiquitous hills that framed everything with their pine and oak and maple forests. Gone, too, was the lonely road that snaked through the place and the sky above it. There was only a dull, noiseless darkness. Staring hard toward the road, she thought she could see figures moving about. She walked around the lot until she found her car parked along with two trucks, next to the store. Somebody had moved it away from the pump. It was under maybe ten inches of snow. She found the keys in the ignition and sat on the cold plastic seat and started it. It came to life easily, the exhaust muted now by the snow. She found the ice scraper under some trash in the back, and got it out to clean the windshield.

Someone—it could only have been Doreen—called at her from the house, but her words died in the distance between the two of them and Samantha slammed the door and put the car in gear. Near the road, she could see the outline of the wreck, the figures standing around, the motionless carcasses of the truck and buggy.

She turned opposite the direction she had come from that morning. She gassed her car hard enough so that she fish-tailed a little, pushing it hard through the snow. A plow had gone through once, a very long time before, and only for that could the car move at all; there was easily four inches on the road still. The Rabbit's engine growled against the task.

She traveled Furnace Road for an hour or more. Eventually the snowfall diminished and a half-moon emerged from behind some clouds to the west, its light neither bright nor gloomy. The sickness had not lifted, despite the afternoon of rest, and Samantha felt a low-level pain in her abdomen that she leaned in to and did her best to ignore.

She passed dozens of farms, a great many of them Amish, all recognizable by their spartan buildings. At the head of the lanes to these stood large, roughly-hewn mailboxes. The houses themselves generally had dim candlelight glowing from some window or another. For the longest time, the road did not stray from this broad valley whose name Samantha did not know.

The radio gave reports of heavy snow and litanies of closings and cancellations and postponements. Chanceyville's schools. A VFW-DAV dance in Chesterton. A 4-H program on rug design in Folsom Summit. All area varsity and JV sports. The list was endless and was repeated when it had been gone through so as to further the sense of its infinity.

She drove through miles of alternating forests and rugged, houseless rangeland, as many as fifteen or twenty. She passed a sign for Weston that was antiquated and rusted—almost homemade-looking, the kind of sign no longer posted anywhere. It said the distant town was either 25 or 28 miles away; it was hard to tell in the light.

Later, she saw a sign that read *Leaving Parson County, Entering Hendricks County*. She knew these county names from a seventh grade Ohio history test in which she'd had to memorize all eighty-eight, but that was the extent of her knowledge of them.

She entered Hendricks County's freshly plowed roads with a jolt, as a plane landing roughly. The cleared road immediately acted to accelerate the Rabbit, and before she could consider how to respond, she had braked hard and the car slid recklessly on the thin layer of snow. She swung the steering wheel in wild, sweeping motions, and was able to navigate the thin corridor between the snow banks this way, but the car swam until the balding tires unexpectedly gripped a patch of asphalt and there was the loud static of rubber on wet rock followed by a loud snap. She stopped. The steering wheel was unresponsive.

She feared the worse, and when she got out, she saw that it was so. The left front wheel had snapped off and was lying on its side as if a pillow for the front axle. The car sat almost perfectly in the middle of the road.

No, she whispered.

She surveyed the country around her. Not a light shone in any direction other than that from a jet thirty-thousand feet overhead.

She was on a small knoll and could see how the land dropped off below her, forming a long, empty pasture, and beyond that, a creek probably, and then a tree line, which climbed out of the bottomlands up a large ridge that seemed to go on indefinitely up and down the road.

She found a flashlight under the passenger seat and shone it on the broken wheel, as if there were something to miss in a tire that had completely snapped off. The snow crunched loudly under her boots, and it seemed that perhaps the clouds had been somehow insulating the country, for now that they were gone, she was cold, and a whip of wind blew down from the north as if to affirm this notion.

Back in the car, she sat and let out a sigh. She started the car back up and turned on the heater and felt its warm air again.

What do you do? she wondered. She tried to remember the road that she had passed over, where things had been—farms, houses, roads. She didn't remember passing a house in a very long time. How far a walk could it be? Her mind felt empty. It was as if she'd never been anywhere but here. She looked at the blue dash clock. It read 7:05.

No FM stations came in. She spanned the dial a couple times—not even a crackle of loud static. Switching to AM, she was able to find one clear channel broadcast from God knew where, on which a sporting event was playing. She didn't care. It was fine, whatever it was, and sitting back in the seat, she didn't know for the longest time—until someone scored a goal—that it was hockey and that it was broadcast out of Chicago. She listened, soothed by the voices of the announcers: "Clark moves across the midline, passes to MacArthur. He's matched up by Antoine Holly, the rookie out of Michigan Tech. Holly bumps MacArthur...."

They might have been speaking Athabascan. The less she understood, somehow, the better. She fell asleep again then, the broken-down Rabbit idling, the heater on high, the radio noise gradually fading into a staccato nothingness in her mind.

She awoke when the car ran out of gas. The clock read 10:18. She had the heavy-headed sensation of someone who has slept either too much or too little and she was consumed with thirst. She got out of the car and picked up a pile of snow with her mitten and ate it. It wasn't good enough—it stung the spots where she'd had fillings and it yielded little water.

Fresh snow swept across the road in places and formed high drifts up against the banks. She surveyed the clearing below her where a stream surely ran, and then got into the car and dug around in the trash behind the front seat until she found an empty Yankee Burger soda cup she thought she'd seen there. It was crushed, but she unfolded it and it seemed like it might still hold water. She tucked her pants into her boots, retightened her boot laces, and she scaled the barbed-wire fence, positioning her feet as close as possible to the flimsy pine posts where the wire was stapled.

In the pasture on the other side, there were no cattle nor anything else living that she could see, not counting a handful of crows perched on nearby trees that seemed impervious to the weather. She began post-holing down the hill toward the dark tree line, the snow soaking her jeans to just below her knees.

The work was slow going, but she made progress. Soon she was on flat ground. She came to a large tree that lay on its side, the top of which sat just above the snow. She crawled over it because it was in her path now and it seemed that it would take less energy to climb it than go around. Soon, she came to a cutbank and could see the creek below. She fought her way through a grove of briars and then slid down the bank to the channel.

She dug around in the snow until she found a large, pointed rock and sought out a likely spot to dig. She cleared snow off the top of the creek with her hands and when she had reached the ice, she began chipping at it. She was desperate to get to the water, spearing ferociously, and could almost feel it running beneath her. This noise reverberated loudly up and down the channel.

When she finally broke all the way through the ice, she found only an air-pocket underneath. She abandoned the spot and scooted out toward the creek's center and repeated the process. She was aware of the danger in this, but didn't see another way around it; she had never been so thirsty.

After just three jabs, she heard the hollow gurgle she sought and could see that the creek was not at all deep. She cleared away enough ice to get a cup into the stream, where it filled slowly. She lifted it to her mouth and drank deep gulps of the sandy water. When she finished, she filled it twice more and drank those, too.

She was panting now, sitting on her knees in the snow. It was dead quiet. For a brief moment, alone in the creekbed, she felt a strange order to all that had happened. The irony of being in the creekbed did not escape her.

If it were questions she'd been asking—or had wanted to ask—she was out of them now. She might even have been prepared to accept some truths—that rivers flowed in one direction only, or that a boy's death mattered, always. But as quickly as these things came to her, her mind whirled against them still, a wind itself. The only truth she could come back to was the cold's indifference, which was beginning to seep into her now.

She knew the cold could easily pull the life from her. It had happened millions of times over millions of years—to people, to wooly mammoths, to trees. There was nothing unique about such a death. Four times in the last billion years, ice had crawled down the northern hemisphere and swallowed everything, had taken the life from nearly everything in its path. And so how was it, knowing this, that one could mourn a single lost life—the life of a Stevie Lowe? The life of a Samantha Longstreth?

11.

Neither the dim light of dusk nor the snow itself give Nate pause. He emptied himself into the snowy world before him, well beyond the boundaries of any of his brother's maps. He didn't really care where he was. He drove for hours this way.

Out here, the long valleys were a mile wide and even in the dark and snow, he could see the road and the stream, dual serpents, inching through the landscape. It all invited him in and he entered with abandon, his father all the while returning to him somehow, the deferred grief slowly bleeding into him so that now he could almost imagine his father sitting next to him, directing him. Take this road, turn here. His father knew every road in southeast Ohio, had taught Nate to drive on roads like these—perhaps they'd driven on this very one, the two of them.

Sometime late that evening, Nate ran out of gas. He had lost track of such details. He got out and walked to find a gas station. The first one he came to was closed—had been since six p.m., according to a sign on the door. He walked on. For an hour, he marched through the deep snow. He didn't care. He found an open station and bought a plastic can and filled it, made the same walk back.

It was well after midnight when he returned to the car and got it running. He traveled on, due south, now on Furnace Road. A cleared sky revealed the shape of the country: it was empty and beautiful and, when he got out of the car once to pee alongside the road, he felt the bitter cold of the place. There, next to him, was a decrepit sign for Weston. He stared at it. Weston, 28 Miles, it read, snow piled up beneath it. He went to his car and dug around for a small toolbox he kept. He pulled out some wrenches and tried two or three until he found the right one, and he unscrewed the sign from its metal post. He took it down and leaned it against the rear quarter panel of his car. A souvenir. His father had surely once read that very sign, he thought.

He put it in the back seat and drove on. Southward, always southward, like it was some panacea for the rising grief. He passed only a few houses out there, and not much in the way of towns or outposts. Sometime not long before daybreak, he saw the first sign of life he'd come across in many hours: a car in the middle of the road with the door open. He stopped to see what was the matter.

Weather

IT WAS GOING TO BE MY BIRTHDAY in a few days and I decided enough was enough. Let's say I didn't feel exactly present. I told Melanie on the way back to her parents' house that I wanted to break it off. I'll be the first to admit that it must have seemed capricious.

Sure enough, she seemed a little dumbfounded at first, sitting over in the passenger seat. But then something appeared to sink in and by the time we'd snaked our way back to her town, she told me she thought it had been inevitable, which was a way of thinking about it I hadn't bothered to reach. I generally did not see the world so absolutely as evitable and inevitable, possible and impossible.

"You're not planning on driving all the way home now, Donnie."

I was quiet.

"You should spend the night," she said. "It's not safe."

The truth, of course, was that I wanted to be out of there, but I was tired and it was a two-hour drive back to Junction City, and it was already nearly two in the morning. I could have slept some alongside the road, I thought, and then gone on, but I figured, why not just sleep here and get up early, be gone before anyone rises.

When I said goodnight to her, she spoke softly, a little sadly, but this manner was not awfully different from her usual manner.

I slept soundly on her older sister's bed in the basement, where I had slept the other nights I'd stayed at her parent's house, and I woke early, well rested despite the brief sleep and the events of the previous night.

I found a note under my door with my name on it as I was dressing and I picked it up and put it in my pocket without unfolding it. When I opened the door, Melanie lay there, too, curled up, asleep, one of those four-color pens and some cream-colored stationery next to her limp hand.

I crept past her—she didn't stir, whether asleep or embarrassed, I didn't know or care—and carefully made my way upstairs. The early sun came through a large window over the breakfast nook and brightly lit the kitchen. I stole a bagel and banana from the counter.

I thought I was away, already mentally going through the music selections in my car when I saw her dad in the driveway, washing his Cutlass Ciera. It wasn't even seven yet.

"Did a real number in there," he said.

"Is that what you call it?"

"Well," he said, pausing dramatically. "What's your next conquest?"

He was a bit of a pill—a bitter man. Kind of an asshole, actually. An English teacher at Melanie's high school in Horace, Kansas. A Dodger fan. Would sit there in front of the TV all damn night cheering on those hapless fools.

"You prefer that I marry her and live unhappily for forty years?" I asked him.

This seemed to cut to the quick.

"Look, Cassanova. You can play by your rules if you want. Just keep in mind that every dog has its day."

He used an awful lot of clichés for an English teacher. "That must mean something," I told him, though I knew very well what it meant.

He answered me anyway. "You'll get bit by your own medicine someday is what it means," he said. Needless to say, I found Mr. Montgomery to be unpleasant, even in good times. These were not good times, not between us anyway.

"Look," I said. "I'm sorry I've hurt your daughter. She'll be okay I think. It's not like I've left her at the altar."

"True," he admitted, but then, as if his inner struggle with all of this were right on the surface, he said, "Just for the record, I never liked you."

"You really find it necessary to tell me that?"

He shrugged. What a wiener.

"Fortunately for me, Mr. Montgomery, your opinion doesn't hold much sway outside that house."

He was getting mad.

"Get out of here," he said. "And leave that banana and bagel. Those are mine. Go earn your own food."

"Sure," I said, and threw them on the dewy lawn. I got into my rusted out Chevelle.

"I never liked you either," I yelled out the window. Obviously it didn't matter how far we took it.

"I don't give a good goddamn what you think," he yelled back, aiming the hose nozzle in my direction, only the water didn't quite reach me. I turned on my windshield wipers just for fun.

"You don't need to bother coming back," he said. He put his thumb over the nozzle so he could get a real taut stream of water, but I was just ahead of him and had my window up by the time he got it straightened out toward my head. It splashed against the window. I goggle-eyed him as I drove off.

I was nearly to the highway when my car gradually lost power and, after a little sputtering, stalled. I tried it six or seven times, but it was done for—wouldn't even turn over.

I got out and walked back to town, which took the better part of half an hour. It was already getting hot. I found a service station in Horace called Ray's Shell. I loitered by the front door for twenty minutes until Ray showed up and I explained my situation to him. He nodded while he put on coffee, smoked a cigarette, opened the cash register and counted the money. Eventually, two more guys appeared, and Ray called one of them over.

"Earl," he said. "This gentleman broke down out toward the reservoir. You take him out there in the tow and get his car—at least see if you can figure out what the deal is."

"Yep," Earl said, sleepy-eyed.

"Follow him," Ray instructed.

I did. The wrecker we took was vintage 1964. It merely had a chain and a lift bar—none of the bells and whistles of the contemporary models; none of those handy lift ramps.

"Probably gonna be blistering today," Earl observed.

I sat quietly.

"I'm Earl Turner," he said.

"Donnie Holland."

"You live around here?" he asked.

"No. Down to Junction City. I have a girlfriend up here."

"Who's that?"

I rattled off the first girl's name I could think of. "Name's Kate."

"Kate . . . ?"

"Holcomb," I said, only afterward realizing that I had conflated the names of two previous girlfriends: Kate Lowe and Mindy Holcomb.

"Don't know her," he said.

"She's not lived here long," I told him.

He nodded.

It didn't take us long to reach the car. He got in and tried it, then took a quick look under the hood.

"Alternator's probably dead," he said. "Killed the battery."

We towed it back to town and he talked to Ray for a while. Ray disappeared into the garage with my car for nearly an hour. Eventually, he came back outside and smoked a cigarette. I was out there sitting on the ground, leaning against the glass window of the office.

"It's your alternator," he said. "I an get one in from Topeka this afternoon, but we ain't got nothing around here for it. Not even rebuilt."

"How much?"

"Hundred and sixty-five or so with labor."

"Shit," I said, shaking my head. I didn't have a lot of spare change for new alternators.

"I'd appreciate it if you'd not swear," he told me.

"Sorry," I said, feeling a little foolish.

"Well, what do you wanna do?"

"Yeah," I said. "I'm going to be needing the car."

"Roger," he said, as in aye-aye, and turned and walked back inside.

I walked down the block to a diner and ate some bacon and eggs. I stayed for a long time and read all of the morning paper, drank a lot of coffee. Nothing of note had happened in the world. There was a big drug bust in Florida and there was a picture of some Feds standing in front of a yacht-looking thing full of what were apparently clear bags of cocaine. There had been flooding in Bangladesh, and there were awful pictures of that, too. And here in the U.S. the governor's convention was going on in Missouri and there were a bunch of these guys mouthing platitudes on the ozone layer. Also the Dodgers lost to the Padres in ten innings, which gave me a silly sense of satisfaction.

When I came back to the station, I positioned myself in a shady spot in the grass away from the noise of the auto-bay. I covered my head with the paper like characters are always doing in old Laurel and Hardy movies and I fell asleep.

Later, I woke up when the sun fell on me; it was one of those hazy Plains days in which the horizon and the clouds sort of mesh, gradually dispelling the idea that there's anything separating them.

I lay there and stared up into the sky for a long time, just spacing. Then I started to think about what I was going to do when I got back to my apartment. I couldn't think of one thing, actually, and imagined I would be doing something very similar to what I was doing here, and thus came to the conclusion that, except for the money, this wasn't all that inconvenient. While I was lying there, Ray appeared over me.

"You awake," he said.

"Yep."

"Listen. I've gotta send Earl over to Vansickle County to pick up a wrecked bug. If you're interested, I'd pay you eight dollars an hour to go with him and help him when he needs it. Might not be anything to do, but it would save me having to send one of my mechanics. You wouldn't be more 'an a couple hours and by then we'll probably have that car of yours up and running."

"Sounds like a fine deal," I told him.

"He'll be leaving here just after lunch. You plan on eating anything?"

"I'll just grab a sandwich," I said. "Take me five minutes."

I had a sandwich made at the same diner and while they made it, I called my CO on my calling card and told him that I'd had car trouble and wouldn't be able to make it on time this afternoon.

"Goddammit, Holland," was all he said, and then hung up.

Earl liked to talk about baseball. One of his son's played in a youth league and so I heard all about that. He was upset about the game dying and thought that kids today cared more about clothes than playing ball, which was the first I'd heard that particular slant. Next came soccer. "A fuckin' communist sport," he told me. Once they brought soccer in wholesale, he figured, we'd have our very own politburo soon enough. I kept my mouth shut on these topics. Earl seemed a smart enough guy who took things just a step further than he should have when he had a captive audience.

"What do you do down to JC?" he asked me.

"I work on the base," I said.

"Civilian?"

"No."

We fell quiet. The radio fizzed. Occasionally I could make out some distant Motown.

"How do you like it?"

"The Army?"

"Yeah."

"It's alright," I said. "I don't love it."

I waited for him to tell me how long he'd been at this job and all that, but he didn't say anything else.

We entered Vansickle County. It was way up there, tucked away in a part of the state I'd not seen before, and I took note of the place and stacked it against the rest of the state and country that I got to know in the few years I'd been there. Earl lit a cigarette and offered me one, which I turned down.

After a number of turns onto unmarked roads, I asked Earl how he was navigating exactly.

"Like a bird, captain," he said, enigmatically. I didn't press the issue. I guess if you live your life in one place, you eventually learn your way around.

Soon we came onto the wreck scene, a semi and a VW bug, both badly mangled on one of these minor state routes, the kind that had maybe been a prominent thoroughfare before World War II, but had gradually become less important as the interstate system went in. A deputy sheriff stood directing traffic.

The bug blocked part of the road, and what little traffic there was eased by in the one open lane; the semi lay on its side in the first few rows of some soybeans as if asleep. It had taken out a hefty-looking fence in getting there.

We pulled up next to the deputy.

"Anyone dead?" Earl asked.

"Naw," the deputy said. "Couple broken bones probably. How you gonna do this?"

Earl surveyed the situation, noting the disfigurement of the car's front end. "I'll pull it from the back to get it out of there, and then I'll set her down and switch it around for the drive home," he said.

The deputy nodded and we positioned ourselves.

We rigged up the axle to the lift and then Earl slowly levitated the car with the hydraulic controls on the side of the truck. He had me get in the cab then and pull it forward and to the side of the road, to where we could get an angle on it, and then he set it down like he'd said, and got back into the truck and maneuvered around to the other side of it and picked it up again. The VW was pretty torn up and hard to situate in a way that would keep it from pulling to the right, but we got it to where Earl was satisfied, more or less.

The deputy started brooming off the road then.

"You all have an awful lot of these sorts of mishaps down this way," Earl said.

"I know it," the deputy said. "Had a godawful storm couple hours back. I reckon one or the other of 'em lost their way in the rain."

"Shit happens, eh?" Earl observed.

"Sure does," said the deputy.

"How's come we get called and not a wrecker from Carthage?" Earl asked. We were sitting in the middle of the road. Earl absently pulled out a cigarette with his two hands resting on top of the steering wheel while he talked to the man.

"Only wrecker in Carthage got his license suspended for DUI."

"Ah. And whose mess is this to clean up?" Earl asked, thumbing toward the eighteen-wheeler.

"Mack is sending some people all the way from KC to take care of it."

Earl rogered that and they talked some more and then we pulled away, headed toward Horace County.

"What's your girlfriend do down here?" he asked some time later.

"She works at a Ponderosa Steak House."

"Good food," he said.

"But she goes to school over to Manhattan."

"You two planning on getting married, then?"

"Probably not," I said.

The sky began to darken and Earl observed we were probably going to get some weather. He turned on the radio—said he wanted to see what sort of news on the situation could be scared up.

"You married?" I asked.

"Seventeen years," he said.

"You don't look old enough for all that."

"Just barely," he told me.

"What's your wife's name?"

"Collette."

"How many kids?"

"We got three, all told. The oldest one's a junior at Horace High."

We rattled along and every seven or eight miles or so, Earl pulled over and we checked on one of the straps that held the car in place because it had dry rot and was threatening to break.

"Ray's been saying for ages he was going to replace this," he explained to me. "But he never does and it just keeps getting worse."

"Things get in the way sometimes," I observed.

"I reckon they do," he said, "but he's going to have bigger bills to pay than a new strap if he don't take care of this soon."

The storm moved in swiftly and overtook us before we'd taken too much notice of it. Eventually, the radio reported tornadoes touching down in three of the five neighboring counties. Not five minutes after this announcement, we saw our very own tornado. It hung in the sky eerily to the south of us, though we couldn't tell in what direction it moved. I'd never seen one before and thought it one of the most ominous things I'd ever seen, almost sort of evil, which I know doesn't make any sense.

"*This* is a damn mess," Earl said. "I can abide all sorts of things, but I do not care for tornadoes."

"Should we pull off?"

"Well, hell yes we should pull off," he said. "But you've got to find someplace safe first. You let me handle things here."

I said nothing. It made sense. I didn't know anything about tornadoes. Where I came from in Ohio, we rarely had tornadoes, whether that was because of the hilly nature of the region or some other more complicated meteorological phenomenon, I didn't know.

We turned off the county road and drove a half mile on gravel before coming to a bridge. By then the rain was making it hard to see anything and the thunder and wind had ratcheted things up considerably. We stopped just short of the bridge, pretty much right in the middle of the road; there were steep banks on either side, but no where else to put the truck and the bug.

"Let's wait it out," he told me.

Everything I'd heard about tornadoes seemed to be true. They are loud like trains and this noise alone is terrifying. Also—and I don't know the science of it—but something changes about the very color of the sky, too; it turns a spooky, jaundiced hue, something much different than your average thunderstorm.

For a moment I believed the tornado was going to take us and the bug and the wrecker and probably the bridge too and send us all back over to Horace County or beyond. Earl seemed to comprehend this and he grabbed my shirt with one hand and the bag containing my sandwich with the other, shut the door with his elbow, and guided me toward the bank. We slid down the incline and waded through dense weeds and hid below the bridge.

There, we heard trees crack and fall and their branches being thrashed around in the swollen creek, but all in all, it was more hospitable than above after you got used to the darkness and the gurgling of the water. We settled on a dry spot above the creek's banks where there was plenty of space. It looked like this had been a hangout for some local kids, equipped with a fire pit and sitting stones and faded graffitied walls.

I found a concrete block and sat on it and Earl handed me my sandwich and told me to eat it, and not altogether kindly. I wasn't much up for eating the sandwich, but I did as he said. He crouched nearby and lit a cigarette. Rainwater blew in some on us.

"So what went wrong with you and your little girl?" He had to talk loudly to be heard.

It was an obvious ploy to get us off the tornado, but I didn't mind. Normally I would have played dumb, but it didn't matter what Earl knew. It really didn't matter what anyone knew. I didn't have any answers to any questions about my girlfriend, Melanie, or a number of other topics that related directly to my existence.

"Usual," I said. I bit into the sandwich. I'd gotten a BLT.

"Which is?"

"Which is I've not got a clue," I told him.

He seemed to me the very bastion of calm.

He laughed. "You'll get used to not having a clue," he told me.

"I'd rather not," I told him.

"You don't got to," he said. "But if you want to, you get used to it."

I didn't say anything to that.

"Course you can just chuck the whole thing, I guess," he said, "but then where are you?"

"That's sort of the plan at the moment," I said.

He thought on that for a minute.

"I mean, I can see that way of thinking."

We watched the wind snap off a twenty foot branch upstream a ways. The water pulled a discarded clothes dryer along as if it were made of airtight plastic.

We sat quiet for a long time, and the noise of the storm subsided slowly and eventually I got over my fright. We waited there for nearly half an hour until it seemed to have passed completely and the sky had lightened some.

"I suppose we should mosey back to town," he said, putting out his fifth cigarette.

"Alright."

Back up top, tree limbs were strewn everywhere, but the truck and bug looked untouched. From where we stood—this being summer and the trees densely foliaged—we couldn't see too much in the way of real damage, and couldn't discern if the tornado had passed close by or not.

"This CB used to work, but it don't anymore," Earl said, seemingly by way of apology. "Else I'd call in and tell Ray the situation."

We headed up the road and found a spot to turn around, which was tricky with the bug on back in such a narrow road. Several times we had to stop while I cleared away fallen tree limbs. Once we got back to the main road, I remembered I'd left a bag of things on the floor of Melanie's sister's room. I closed my eyes: how could I have forgotten my bag at that house? I might have done without it and all its contents, but inside there was a watch that had belonged to my father. I wore it even though it was junky and about forty years old because I didn't have much else to remember him by. It did a poor job of telling time and did so with little sliding digits like most watches use only for the date.

When we got back to Horace, I asked Earl to drop me four blocks from Melanie's house and told him I'd be at the shop in less than an hour to pick up my car.

I made my way to the backside of the house through a wooded path Melanie had taken me on that ran adjacent to the high school where her dad taught, and where she herself had graduated two years earlier.

The whole Montgomery clan was supposed to be down to Topeka today, at Melanie's little brother's cello debut, which was happening at some arts institute. The next Yo-Yo Ma, they thought.

I'd never broken into a house. I knew that the Montgomerys didn't lock their back door, though, so it wouldn't be messy, and I would be in and out in no time, and on my way home.

Inside it was quiet. I stood animal-like for a moment, waiting to hear movement. I heard none. In and out, I repeated to myself quietly. No lingering. No bananas. None of those little star crunches her mom always fed to me, though now that it came to mind, I was still a little hungry; I had a bit of a sweet tooth. I saw on the cuckoo clock that it was just before three o'clock and reminded myself not to jump when the clock performed its ritual.

In the faux paneled and carpeted basement, the potpourri scent could not quite disguise the dank, earthy smell. This was a basement and it was moist, just a half step removed from the earth itself.

Melanie's sister had been in band, like Melanie and their little brother Kale, and there were trophies and photos all around of those halcyon days. Camille—the sister—hugging two other girls in front of—what was it?—the Jefferson Memorial? Camille holding her clarinet to her mouth and looking toward the camera.

I found my bag where I'd left it and snatched it up, robber-like, and bolted upstairs toward the back door. But then I remembered Melanie curled up outside my door that morning and I decided to look to make sure everything was in order. I rummaged around the bag and noticed nothing out of the ordinary at first. Then my pulse raced. The watch, I thought. The watch itself was missing. It was a worst case scenario. What had she done with my dad's watch?

I dumped the bag out on the kitchen floor and spread out all the contents. No watch. Maybe I had left it somewhere, I thought. I reconstructed the night before. Pizza Hut. The Harrison Ford movie. The party with her high-school friends. The drive along the reservoir home. There was no place it could be, but either on my wrist or in my bag, and at last, I remembered putting it there, carefully, while I was lying in bed, a copy of Steinbeck's *The Winter of Our Discontent* resting on my chest (I'd found the Reader's Digest Condensed version on Camille's shelf).

I went back downstairs and looked around the room again. No watch. Back upstairs. I peered around the den, Melanie's bedroom. There was a picture of the two of us in a frame there. She worked quickly; we had only been dating for a few months. I searched the rest of the house, the bathroom, the cupboards, the vegetable drawer in the fridge. Why are you looking in the vegetable drawer, I thought vacantly. Nobody even puts vegetables there. Except the Montgomerys; their vegetable drawer was chock-a-bloc with iceberg lettuce and old celery and carrots. Not surprisingly, there was no watch.

I looked around. Afternoon light shone in from the front room. The sitting room, these things were called. Nobody ever sat there. There were mints in a dish on a coffee table and I ate two of those. There were more

Readers Digest novels here. And some sort of compendium called Foxfire that my mom had in her sitting room, too. No watch.

I peered cautiously out the front window, drawing the curtains very carefully, not sure what I was looking for. It just seemed like that's the thing the burglar does from time to time—glances out the window to make sure the coast is clear.

There was no one out; it was too hot. Plus, there had been tornadoes in just about every county within a hundred miles, and for all I knew, there were entire sections of Horace leveled. The Montgomerys themselves could have been killed, driving in their Cutlass Ciera toward Topeka. I saw them, lifted up to about 300 feet, their car comically spinning around like one of those little maple seed propellers that fall in the summer. Weirdly, it was Melanie's dad's face that I saw, not hers. He didn't seem able to scream, so he just sat there, seat-belted in, waiting for the end. It was unsettling to see him like that, and to get my mind off it, I made myself think of the Padres beating the Dodgers last night out in California.

I peered around the neighborhood and caught a quick flash of light from the driveway. I squinted. Something glistened brightly there on the concrete.

Aw hell, I said. I opened the door and went out.

It was my watch—my father's watch—crushed. I picked up the pieces and held them in my hand. I considered their weight. Probably he'd bought it at a PX in Brownsville one afternoon all of those years ago, before a big night out. He'd probably shown it all around that night and several other guys had held up their wrists to show theirs—the same watch. Everyone would have had a big laugh and then there would have been more beers brought to the table and some grousing about this or that commanding officer. There would have been girls involved somehow, local girls, the grown children of majors and sergeants from the base, girls whose futures were uncertain, but most likely involved marrying an Airman First Class and eventually moving with him to his hometown in Oregon or Ohio.

And now my father was gone, and probably some of those other guys were gone, and the girls, too, some of them were gone. Brownsville probably wasn't the same—or if it wasn't Brownsville, then Roswell, or Colorado Springs. It didn't matter; they were all different places now. Had to be. People and things were always changing, disappearing, going away, dying, drifting off, slipping back into the ground. It seemed the only truth of being alive. I put the watch in my pocket.

On the concrete, written in a pastel chalk—an orange the color of those ice cream pushups—it said, "We're not quite even, but I feel a little better."

I knew this wasn't Melanie's work. It was her dad's. What a loon, I thought. It was spooky imagining him doing this in the hopes that I would come back and see it.

The neighborhood was perfectly still. I thought for a moment about what I might do to retaliate. I can't lie; I considered several heinous acts, the most devious of which was pissing in his favorite Dodger-watching chair.

In the end, I didn't do any of those things. A guy like me, I realized, would always lose in a battle against a guy like him; he knew exactly what he was after and he was going to get it; he was going to persist and fight against everything and eventually he was going to prevail somehow, and that, above all else, was probably the most important distinction between the two of us.

That old watch, I knew, didn't represent my dad anymore than his gravestone or the photos of him in Myrtle Beach or his old letters or even the stories I told about him. This was merely an old crushed watch that he had once owned. I decided to leave the watch for Melanie's dad and reached into my pocket to retrieve it, and accidentally pulled out with it the piece of paper I'd forgotten about—the note from Melanie. Why not go ahead and get all this over with at once, I thought. I threw the watch down and opened the note. It was damp from the rain and sweat, but legible. God knows how many drafts it took her, but it contained just one line—four words, all told. *I wish you well*, it said. That was it. *Love, Melanie.* It touched me that she would decide to tell me just this one thing, and for a moment, I felt pretty small and wished I could touch her hand and show her that I was human, that I felt, that I wished her well, too. I did wish her well.

I turned and started on my way back to Ray's Shell then and the heat came down and blanketed me. I had a lot on my mind, I suppose, but soon the heat took it all away, one of those rare little gifts you get from the world that come along at precisely the right moment.

I just walked and for those forty-five minutes there was nothing but certainty. I took off my shirt and wrapped it around my head, turban-style. No one was out. It was a Tuesday in the middle of July, and really hot now—98 degrees, according to the Farmers and Merchants Bank on Wood Street. I had survived my first tornado today. Who knew what else I would survive.

Reagan's Army
in Retreat

I AWOKE IN THE MORNING to the sound of a hunting knife—a Bowie, I knew, when I saw the large blade—cutting right through the top of my tent. A small pile of snow fell on me and a bearded, barrel-chested man in a camo-jacket stood over the tent, silhouetted by an overcast sky.

"What in the hell you think you're doing, chief?" he said.

"Huh?"

"You best have some answers better than *huh*," he told me.

I couldn't see the man too well, the light behind him making him mostly shadows.

"Donnie?" I said.

"No, not Donnie."

"Hold on a second," I said, starting to get a picture of the situation. "I think there's just been a misunderstanding."

"Buddy, where I stand this here's more in the realm of major fuck up."

"Yes," I said. "I'll clear it all up in a sec. You won't need that thing out though."

"I'll put it away soon enough," he said. "You got one minute." He pulled back the sleeve of his coat to examine a large watch.

I sat up. "You live here, I guess?" I could see him now. He was not my brother—much heftier than Donnie, not at all the right demeanor.

"That's right, genius," he said. "I live here."

"You know Donnie Holland?"

"What's Donnie Holland have to do with your butt playing Boy Scout in my wife's flower garden?"

"Donnie's my brother."

"Chief," he said, "that's a problem well beyond my control."

"I thought this was his yard," I said.

"It ain't."

"I can see that," I said.

"Used to be."

"Yeah?"

"What do you want here?"

"I came into town late during the storm," I told him. "I looked up Donnie, came here, and there was no answer. I didn't have anyplace to go, so I set up a tent."

"Some people work," he said. "We go to bed early."

"I'm sorry," I told him. "I'll get my stuff out of here."

"You're *Donnie's* brother?" he asked, incredulous.

"That's right."

"You don't look a thing like him."

I shrugged.

"He don't live here no more," he said.

"Got it."

"I mean, he don't live in JC no more. Moved down to Texas last year. That's an old fucking bag there." He had bent down and was feeling the material of my sleeping bag like it was Thai silk. "What is that, Korean Era?"

"Yeah," I said. "My father's."

"You don't see them much."

I was out of the sleeping bag now and had my boots on. There was nothing left to do but stand up, right through the hole he'd created. Standing, I could see a world of white in all directions, the murky dawn behind it. In the picture window of the house stood the rest of the man's family, a youngish woman and two kids, a boy and a girl.

"You get your stuff packed up and you come inside and have some food," he said.

"That's all right," I said. "I need to be pushing off."

"No," he said firmly. "You come inside for some eggs. I apologize for the bellicosity, but a lot a weird shit goes down around here. I'll find you another tent out in the garage—got a box of them fuckers somewhere."

I did as he said. I was cold to the bone and wasted little time being neat with the tent, wadding it up in a ball and shoving it in the empty spare tire well.

The door of the small house opened onto the living room, where the man's wife was stoking a wood-burning stove, the kind my grandmother used to have—one that you can cook on and bake in, though this one was in the living room. The room was already unbearably warm, and the contrast from the cold outside made me a little faint for a moment.

"Hi," she said. "I'm Carol. This here's Toby and Netty." She pointed to two children sitting in chairs at a table in the next room.

The man reappeared after a minute, holding a brand new camouflage tent bag still in a clear plastic outer cover. He briefly observed it as if it were a large piece of rotten fruit, and then handed it to me. "What's your name?" he asked.

"Nate Holland."

"I'm Brett Mills," he said and grabbed my hand. "Nate here is brothers to old Donnie," he told his wife. "Thought Donnie still lived here. That's why the camp-out."

Carol nodded slowly and seemed to hide a grin. "I got some breakfast on the table," she said.

"Ah shit," Brett said, holding his head askew, grimacing. "I ain't got time. I got to be over to Dwight's and help him load up that bed and dresser."

"Well take some bacon or something with you," Carol said.

"I'll get something later." He kissed her and then the kids and then made his way for the door, stopping briefly to scrutinize me again. "I reckon it's safe to leave the brother of old Donnie Holland alone with my family," he said, not really to anyone but himself, and then he opened the door to the front yard. I could see the large sheath of the knife at his side. "I hope you have some luck finding that old boy," he said over his shoulder. "He's crazy as a shithouse rat. In Amarillo or some damn place."

"Thanks," I said, now at the door myself. There wasn't any need explaining that I wasn't looking for my brother exactly. "I appreciate the tent."

"Late Christmas," he said, and then he was gone, and there was, in fact, something aloof and Santa-like about him.

"Sit down there," Carol said, indicating a large mound of scrambled eggs on the table, a gallon container of orange juice, and some dried-out microwaved bacon.

"You like some toast?"

"That's okay," I told her. "This'll do fine."

I hungrily ate all the food on my plate. The kids—both somewhere in the vicinity of ten—were a little antsy and not too interested in their food; the boy had a book he half hid under the table and stole glances at until his mother told him to put it down and eat. I saw when he put it down that it was *The Son of Tarzan*.

School had been canceled, Carol told me, and the kids were going to go sledding after breakfast.

"Where do kids go sledding in Kansas?" I asked. The girl, Netty, giggled, though it wasn't clear at what.

"There's places," Carol said smiling a very pretty smile. "The river bluffs. There's a few big hills over there."

"Which river's that?" I asked.

"Three of 'em here," she said. "They'll be going to the Kansas, though."

I nodded.

A long silence followed and I knew it would've been polite to ask something else, but I didn't. For that matter, she probably should've asked me something else, too—what, maybe, had brought me to Junction City in a snowstorm. And how come I didn't know my brother had moved a half year ago? She might have asked where I lived, if I was married, did I have kids of my own? But neither of us said anything and I was a little relieved for it.

She did offer me some more food, which I declined. I got up and refilled my coffee cup at the counter, though, and walked over to the sliding glass doors behind the kids to take a look at the morning forming outside. From there, I could see that the Mills' house more or less marked the end of Junction City Proper. Beyond was an eternity of plains, snow-covered and still at this hour. The sun had finally shown through in earnest and made the snow glisten a little.

For some crazy reason, I imagined the place full of buffalo, which was something I sometimes did when I was traveling through the Plains states. And I imagined, too, my brother standing here and observing his piece of the pie—probably even imagining buffalo himself. It was the kind of thing he was given to; he read westerns and war novels like some kids threw tennis balls against walls, perpetually enacting the scenes in the woods.

There wasn't much out there on the plains: unwanted land mostly, no water, no trees, hardly arable. It stood on the edge of a whole lot of nothingness. But there was something appealing about it, too, and I could easily imagine him with a cup of coffee in his own hand before going in to the meat processing plant—his job last we spoke—and being stirred inside by what he saw there at dawn.

Netty tugged at my sleeve, asking if I wanted to play UNO. She had a deck she'd gotten for Christmas, she said, and maybe we could all play a game now that breakfast was over. I wanted to beg off, to explain that I needed to get on the road to make up lost time. But then we all smelled something burning.

"Mom," Toby said without looking up from his book, which he no longer bothered concealing. "Toast is burning."

The rest of us looked to the toaster, which sat on the countertop, empty. Unplugged even. Carol got out of her chair very quickly and ran toward the living room. I decided to sit at the table and await the news. The kids did the same. Netty looked at me and told me she was nine. Then she giggled and asked me how old I was. When I told her twenty-four, she giggled again and then she yelled into the other room to ask her mom if twenty-four was old.

Instead of replying, Carol was saying "shit" repeatedly in the other room. "Shit. Shit. Shit. Shit."

I got up to go in and see what the problem was, and the kids followed me, Toby reluctantly marking his place in the book with a "Vacation Bible School" bookmark. Soon we were all standing in front of the stove as it issued black smoke into the room. "Jesus," she said. "What's the matter with it?"

"Maybe the flue's shut," I suggested.

"I'm pretty sure it's not."

I reached down and turned the lever, and a huge cloud of smoke puffed from it before I could turn it back. We all coughed, and the kids ran out of the room, screaming, half-playing.

"What you got in there?" I asked.

"Wood," she said. "And paper, to get it going. A little trash. Toilet paper rolls, cereal boxes, a milk carton or two. Should I try to put it out?"

"Yes," I said. "Put it out."

She grabbed a fire extinguisher from the kitchen and fired it into the belly of the stove. In the meantime, I went out into the yard to see if anything was coming from the chimney. Flames, in fact, were coming from it, as was black smoke.

I scuttled back through the yard, up to my knees in the snow and reported what I had seen. "Looks to be in the chimney," I said. Smoke still filled the room, and Carol held a blue phone receiver in her hand.

The kids stood unhelpfully with her in the living room, watching with excited interest, like they might be waiting their turn to bat at softball. Fear had not yet taken hold of them as it had for Carol, who was now talking to the local emergency dispatcher.

I felt something slightly more complicated. I had the benefit of not being involved; I had just met these people not a half hour ago. This house and a hundred others like it could burn down. Entire cities in Kansas or California could be swallowed up by earthquakes or tornadoes and what would it matter to me? I was the dispassionate observer, neutral.

The thought crossed my mind to just leave. I wasn't up for tragedy this morning. It wasn't like they were asleep and in much danger; they would get out. And so I did. I left the camo tent where it rested on the floor and walked out the front door as if I were going to go check on the chimney again. I didn't say anything to the family, and they were already deep enough into the event not to notice my comings and goings.

Outside, it had turned into a bright, cloudy day, and the snow lay brilliant over the yards and cars and rooftops. Fire came from the chimney in droves now, spitting wild flames upward which then disappeared and seemed to have been altogether suppressed before even higher flames replaced them.

Near my car I noticed an elderly man approaching, very slowly, with a wire hair terrier on a leash. He walked in the street, which had been plowed at some late hour—I'd heard the truck from my tent in the night—but there were still several inches of snow on the ground and his feet made dense, crunchy sounds in it. He came right up to me like he knew me. We stood quietly for a moment, observing the chimney.

"This don't look good," he said, shielding his eyes from the rising sun with his arm.

"No. Not good."

"You live here, do you?"

"No. It's the Mills' place."

"Mills?" he said. "They come and go so damn fast anymore, I can't keep up with 'em."

He observed his dog. "Digger," he yelled. "Get away from there." Digger was inspecting the front driver's side tire of my car.

"For years a family named Blankenship lived in this here house," he explained. "Lifer over at Fort Riley. Drill sergeant the likes of which you won't find anymore, I imagine. Served overseas twice, et cetera." Then he began pointing to each house with his cane and naming the families he associated it with. "Colsons there. Martins. Funks. Dells. Timsons." He went right down the block.

"Uh huh," I said. "All gone?" I didn't really know why I was even in this conversation. But he seemed to have lost interest in this train of thought. "Chimney fire, ain't it?" he said.

It felt like we might be observing children ice skating, such was the casualness of his tone.

"I think so. You know what to do about that?"

"Nah," he said. "Call the fire department. That's why we pay taxes."

"Yeah," I said. "Sure."

"You visiting here from Ohio, are you?" he asked, pointing to the license plates on my car with the wooden cane that was starting to seem ornamental.

"That's right," I said.

He nodded. "Excellent football in Ohio. What was it, Hopalong Cassidy. Woody Hayes. That there Archie Griffin. Long history of excellent football."

I nodded.

In another manic shift, he looked around abruptly and got a sour look on his face. "Jesus," he said. "Look at this goddamned place. You got Coloreds and Hispanics all up and down here now." He was shaking his head. "Hell, I don't know. I ain't got nothing against any honest folks. But it just makes me sick to see everything go the way it has is all."

Something about this sad man bothered me a lot.

"I should check on the house," I told him.

He looked up at me. Was it disgust he had for me or some other emotion I hadn't yet seen or felt?

"You ought," he said. "Probably a chimney fire, though. Can't do much but wait on something like that." He seemed like he'd been walking around looking for the opportunity to have this conversation, and now that it was over, he was spent for the day.

"Come on Digs," he said and turned back in the direction he'd come from.

I walked back to the house then, no more aware of a decision to do so than of the day of the week or what exactly was my purpose in the world.

Inside, I saw the rear sliding glass door standing open; Carol and the kids were piling electronics on the deck, in the snow. It was all junk, nothing newer than a decade old—the monitor and disc drive of an early Commodore computer, a Panasonic component stereo from the time when stereos were encased in flashy aluminum. A microwave and toaster oven and a dated boombox with all sorts of useless graphics on the front.

The kids struggled into the kitchen, together hauling a large-screen television far too big for them to carry, swaying under the weight. I took it from their hands and, looking over my shoulder at them, told them to get their coats on and go and stand outside on the back porch and to stay there.

Already the stack of belongings had become significant. I stepped over a hibachi grill and another television and gingerly sat the TV down on the crowded deck and turned to go back inside but met with Carol carrying a half-closed suitcase of clothes. She marched right past me and flung it out as she would have a viper she discovered in her hands. The jettisoned case twisted through the air and then hit the deck banister, spun over the top, and released all its contents before it finally landed in the soft snow.

Only then did we hear the first the sirens echo through town. Carol looked up toward the sound for a moment, but almost immediately turned on her heel and re-entered the house, saying, "Would you pull out the kitchen table?" Before I could respond, Netty was again before me, this time hauling a terrarium with a lizard inside. Behind her the kitchen was getting clouded with smoke.

"I thought I told you to get your coat on and get outside."

She didn't even respond, just held up the terrarium.

"That guy won't last ten minutes outside," I said. "He doesn't have blood like us."

She looked at me like I was the crazy man who inhabited their back porch.

"He was Winston's," she said.

"Who?"

"Winston," she said, pointing at the lizard. Winston, I remembered, was my brother's young son. "His name is Gordon," she said.

"Why didn't Winston take him to Texas?"

She shrugged.

"Put Gordon there, inside the door," I said. "Leave the door open. He'll be okay. The fire department's almost here now. It's all going to be okay."

She did as I said and then started to go back in.

"Ah no," I said. "You stay right here. You've got to promise me you'll stay right here. Promise?"

"I promise," she said.

"It's going to be okay. I'll be right back."

I went inside and saw that the fire had finally burned through the chimney; flames were spreading out around the chimney in the ceiling. It was really going now.

I pulled out the small kitchen table, like Carol had asked, and the four chairs, and then I went in again. The smoke was dense and watered my eyes. I yelled for Carol.

"Here," came a reply from the basement.

I stood at an open door off the kitchen that looked down a flight of stairs.

"You've got to get out of there," I said. "It's going to be okay. The fire department's going to put it out. But we got to get out now."

"There's some stuff down here Brett'd die without."

I quickly lowered myself down the steep steps into the room. It was a half-basement, nearly full of motorcycle equipment—including the rusted bodies of two old Harleys.

"So stupid," she said. "So goddamn stupid." She was sobbing now, nearly ready to crumple into a ball and give in.

"This stuff will be okay, Carol. Smoke damage isn't going to hurt this stuff. It's all okay. Help is here. Where's Toby?"

She shrugged. "I don't know," she cried.

"Let's go," I said. "Get a coat on."

I guided her back up the stairs and outside, where she picked up Netty and the two of them were frozen there in time for a moment, part of an awful painting of tragedy, like some ham-fisted artist's critique of capitalistic society, all their possessions behind them.

I found Toby in his room looking at the top of his closet, which was full of board games. There was nothing in the room for him to use to reach them.

"Come on, bud," I said. "Get a coat on and get outside. I'll get these."

I reached up and brought down as many as I could hold. We were both starting to cough now from the smoke.

"This is a real fucking mess, ain't it?" he said.

I could only answer that yes, it was. And I ushered him down the hallway toward the backdoor.

Outside, the four of us congregated on the large porch. The sirens were loud now.

"It's going to be all right," I repeated, this time to them all. "Everyone's okay. That's the most important thing. They're going to put this out in a hurry."

"The hell they will," Carol cried. "The whole thing is going to burn."

"They're here," I said. "They're right here." I didn't even know how to try to make it okay. And she was right; the place was probably going to go up; flames licked the ridge of the roof as we spoke.

I figured that this might be the end of it for the Mills in Junction

City. Who knew. Probably there wasn't much keeping them here. It'd been the army after all that had brought them, whenever that was. And Brett, like my brother, had clearly left that some time ago. Probably he did plumbing or brickwork or something else that other places needed just as bad. And the Mills would be flung to one of those places now, drawn back to Kentucky or New Hampshire or California, living with family until they could get established. There were tens of thousands like them, I knew, amassed to defend us against the Russians. But now the Peace Corps was in Russia and Reagan's Army had been dispersed.

At about the time the trucks barreled into the yard out front, something next to Toby's foot caught my eye, sitting there half-covered in snow: a plastic robot game my brother and I had owned when we were little. It was a trivia game with its answers on 8-track tapes—the thing didn't even have a computer in it. I picked it up and turned it over and confirmed my suspicions. In faded black marker were our names: Donnie Holland/Nathan Holland.

It startled me, like I'd dug down in the snow and found my brother himself there. Donnie never cared much for the thing, but I had sat for hours on end with it in a small cubby hole in the bedroom we shared, eventually memorizing all the tapes that came with it. "Who was the first man to walk on the moon?" it would ask. "Press A for Buzz Aldrin, B for John Glenn, or C for Neil Armstrong." When you gave the right answer, it said, in its faux computer voice, "That is correct. Would you like to hear Mr. Armstrong's famous words?" If you hit A then, Neil Armstrong's distant, staticky voice came on, repeating his wisdom for the millionth time.

I was lost for just a minute, holding the thing. The family was rushing toward the road, where the fire fighters were already digging out buried hydrants. I put it down and observed it amidst the detritus of the Mills' lives—a collection of things not so different from what I would have to show were my life laid bare this way. Minutes passed. The fire seemed on the brink of completely engulfing the house. When the first water finally hit the flames, the family, I saw, stood huddled together, watching with some mix of hope and despair.

I wanted to console them somehow, but instead I was thinking about my brother and that entirely other life I had lived as a child. In my mind, I saw Donnie leading me through multiflora rose next to a snow-covered creek, guiding me through the imaginary world he inhabited of SS troops and landmines. I was happy to be back with him in that moment, before every inevitable thing that came to pass afterward. In my mind, he was pressed against the white earth in front of me, long weeds popping through the snow all around him. "Stay low, Nate," he was saying. "We're surrounded. Repeat: you've got to stay low and move."

THE AUTHOR

Jerry Gabriel studied at The Ohio State University, Northern Arizona University, and the University of Iowa Writers' Workshop. He has worked as a science writer and taught writing at a number of colleges and universities, including, from 2001-2008, as a lecturer in Cornell University's Engineering Communications Program. Currently he is a visiting assistant professor of English at St. Mary's College of Maryland. His fiction has appeared in *One Story, Epoch, Cimarron Review, Tampa Review*, and *Fiction*, among other magazines, and has been short-listed for a Pushcart Prize. In 2004, he was awarded an artist grant by the New York Foundation for the Arts. *Drowned Boy* is his first book of fiction.